Photo by John Wright

ALESHA DIXON first found fame as part of
Brit-nominated and Mobo Award-winning group Mis-teeq,
which achieved 2 platinum albums and 7 top ten hits,
before going on to become a platinum-selling solo artist in
her own right. Alesha's appearance on *Strictly Come
Dancing* in 2007 led to her winning the series and
becoming a judge for three seasons.

Since then she has presented and hosted many
TV shows including CBBC dance show *Alesha's Street
Dance Stars*, *Children In Need*, *Sport Relief* and BBC1's
The Greatest Dancer. She is a hugely popular judge on

D0542270

ALSO BY ALESHA DIXON,
IN COLLABORATION WITH KATY BIRCHALL

GIRLS RULE

BY

ALESHA DIXON

In collaboration with KATY BIRCHALL

■ SCHOLASTIC

I dedicate this book to the amazing girls who rule our household!
Azura and Anaya, Mummy and Daddy's angels xxx

Published in the UK by Scholastic, 2021
Euston House, 24 Eversholt Street, London, NW1 1DB
Scholastic Ireland, 89E Lagan Road, Dublin
Industrial Estate, Glasnevin, Dublin, D11 HP5F

SCHOLASTIC and associated logos are trademarks and/or
registered trademarks of Scholastic Inc.

Text © Alesha Dixon, 2021
Cover character artwork by Amanda Quartey © Scholastic, 2021

The right of Alesha Dixon to be identified as the author of this work has been
asserted by her under the Copyright, Designs and Patents Act 1988.

ISBN 978 1407 19850 7

A CIP catalogue record for this book is available from the British Library.

All rights reserved.
This book is sold subject to the condition that it shall not,
by way of trade or otherwise, be lent, hired out or otherwise circulated in
any form of binding or cover other than that in which it is published. No
part of this publication may be reproduced, stored in a retrieval system,
or transmitted in any form or by any means (electronic, mechanical,
photocopying, recording or otherwise) without prior
written permission of Scholastic Limited.

DISCARDED

LONDON BOROUGH OF
RICHMOND UPON THAMES

FROM

This
and di
ficti

90710 000 483 310

Askews & Holts | 03-Sep-2021

RICHMOND UPON THAMES

JF TEENAGE 11-14

RTWH | LIBRARY SERVICE

PROLOGUE

"Pearl? Pearl, wake up."

A hand gently nudges me and I bat it away grumpily, burying my face further into the squishy pillow.

"Pearl, it's time to get up," Mum sighs, shaking my shoulder a little more firmly this time. "Come on, rise and shine. It's seven a.m."

I groan as she stands and opens the curtains, letting a stream of bright sunlight into the room. Blinking hazily, I force myself to sit up and let out a loud, pointed yawn. My Cocker Spaniel, Rosy, who was sleeping soundly on the bed next to me, yawns in solidarity before bouncing over to give Mum a good-morning lick.

"You and I need to have words, Rosy," Mum tells her sternly, while giving her a scratch behind the ears. She turns to me, raising her eyebrows. "Have you seen the mess your dog has made?"

Her eyes flicker to the floor, and I crane my neck to have a look, bracing myself for whatever destruction Rosy has caused now. Rosy is my best friend in the whole wide world and, in my opinion, she's *perfect*.

I do have to admit, however, that she has a few . . . well . . . behavioural issues.

There was the time she ripped up the sofa cushions, covering the living room in foam and white fluff, and then she went on to chew through several important-looking wires, destroy the remote control and ruin my favourite backpack. Not to mention the many vases and photo frames she's smashed when she gets overexcited and zooms round the house in an uncontrollable whirlwind, knocking into tables and walls as she goes.

Mum still hasn't forgiven her for chewing her prized Manolo Blahnik red satin heels.

As I peer over the bed to see what trouble Rosy has landed me in this morning, I wince in preparation, hoping that it's nothing too bad, before letting out a sigh of relief when I see what Mum is going on about. My bedroom floor is littered with shredded toilet paper.

"That's fine!" I exclaim, slumping back on my pillow. "It's only a bit of loo roll."

"It is *not* fine," Mum emphasizes, as Rosy gets fed

up of Mum's attention and jumps across the duvet to cover me in slobbery licks, her tail wagging happily. "You need to train her, Pearl. She's getting out of control."

Mum shakes her head at me as I tell Rosy what a good girl she is.

"So, how did you sleep?" she asks, picking some golden dog hairs off her smart black dress.

"Good, I think," I say with a yawn, rubbing sleep out of my eye. "How about you?"

"I didn't sleep *a wink*," Mum says, looking at me expectantly, the corners of her mouth twitching.

At first, I'm confused. Then it hits me.

I remember what day it is. Any sleepiness is gone in an instant as my brain kicks into gear. *HOW HAVE I NOT ASKED HER THE QUESTION YET?* I gasp, sitting bolt upright and leaning forwards to grab her hand.

"Are . . . are the results in?" I whisper, my throat tightening with nerves and excitement.

Mum nods, taking my hand in hers and squeezing it. "Yes. The results are in."

"AND?" I squeak.

A smile spreads across my mum's face, her eyes twinkling.

"Pearl, we did it," she says softly, as though she can't quite believe the words coming out of her mouth. "You are officially looking at the new Prime Minister of the United Kingdom."

CHAPTER ONE

My mum is the Prime Minister. MY MUM IS THE PRIME MINISTER!

I am so happy I could BURST! There is so much to take in, my brain feels like it's about to explode. I feel VERY overwhelmed, but in the BEST WAY.

The Prime Minister! It's the most important job in the COUNTRY! And my MUM has been elected to do it!

This is a BIG deal.

I mean, for anyone it would be a big deal, but it feels even *more* momentous because the odds were stacked against her. She's going to be the first black female Prime Minister this country has had. Wait. She's not *going* to be.

She *is*.

I always knew she could do it. When my mum sets her mind on doing something, then that's it. She gets it done. Even when it seems impossible. Her closest adviser, Sebastian, said last week that even though things were looking good in terms of her support from the public, we shouldn't get our hopes up. *But she did it.*

Is it possible to explode with happiness and pride? Because it kind of feels like that might happen any minute now.

After I scream in excitement, Mum and I do a little celebratory dance. Although, it's not really dancing, because I hate dancing; it's more her bopping hilariously around my bedroom while I jump up and down on the bed, with Rosy going wild, no idea what's happening but pleased to be involved. Mum then stops dancing, collects herself and asks me in her most authoritative voice NEVER to tell anyone that she danced around the room when she found out the news.

"I won't tell anyone while you're in office," I promise her, catching my breath after all the jumping. "But I can't promise to keep it out of my memoirs."

She laughs, gives me a big hug, tells me she loves me and then pulls away, reminding me to go over today's official schedule that her PA, Gabrielle, set out for me in the instance that Mum would win the election.

"I already memorized it," I admit, grinning at her. "I never had any doubt, Mum."

She smiles at me. "Couldn't have done it without you, Pearl. You're my rock."

She then has to leave my room pretty sharpish because, when you're the new Prime Minister, it's not just a question of thanking the public and getting on with the job. There is a LOT you have to do first.

Like, go have a chat with the Queen and stuff.

I am FREAKING OUT. On the inside. Not on the outside, of course. On the outside, I am poised and calm, constantly reminding myself that I am the daughter of the Prime Minister now, and I have to act like it. *I AM THE DAUGHTER OF THE PRIME MINISTER.*

I am SO ready to step into this role.

The first thing I do when Mum leaves the room is jump off the bed and race over to my wardrobe, swinging the doors open and delicately pulling out the hanger with the dress on it that has been chosen for me to wear today. A Stella McCartney design, it's emerald green with a matching belt round the waist that ties into a pretty bow in the middle. It's smart, but not too smart, and grown-up, but not too grown-up. Or at least, that's what my mum's stylist said last week.

Admiring the dress as I lay it down on my bed, I suddenly realize that I won't be sleeping in this bed for much longer. In a few weeks, I won't be in this bedroom. We're moving house.

I'm moving into 10 Downing Street.

"Rosy," I say, trying to get my head round it all as I watch her attack my slippers, "we need to start packing."

She growls at my slipper in reply.

I close my eyes and take a deep breath in through the nose, exhaling through my mouth, just like Mum's yoga instructor has taught me to do whenever I feel overwhelmed. I feel better already.

It's strange. Mum and I have prepared for this moment, she's worked so hard for years for this day to come, and I knew that today was going to change things for ever. But it doesn't feel real. Maybe it will when I'm standing in the hallway of 10 Downing Street, looking around at what will be our new house for the next few years. Maybe that's when it will really kick in.

Oh my goodness. *I am the daughter of the Prime Minister.* I take another deep breath in. I can do this. I am ready for this. I have to behave perfectly and make this transition as smooth as possible for Mum.

"If I'm this overwhelmed, imagine how she's feeling," I say to Rosy, who is too busy barking at my bedside lamp to acknowledge me.

Leaving Rosy to tell my lamp what's what, I head

to the bathroom and hop into the shower, deciding it would be a good idea to run through today's schedule out loud, just to make sure I'm fully prepared. Gabrielle made fun of me yesterday when I told her that I'd made some extra notes, adding in a few small but significant details.

For example, my schedule stated that, in the event Mum won the election, I would be picked up to be taken to Buckingham Palace, but it didn't originally say the name of the driver nor the make and model of the car. It now does, thanks to my notes, so there won't be any confusion about which car is for me.

"You'll know which car is for you, because it will be the only car waiting for you and your mum," Gabrielle said with a bemused smile.

"Actually, I checked and there will also be cars outside for Mum's security detail, as well as for you and Sebastian," I argued smugly. "This way, there can be no confusion."

She laughed. "All right then. You really are the most organized thirteen-year-old I've ever met."

"Thank you! It's like Mum says, if you have everything planned, you're ready for anything."

"Sure." She sighed, giving me a strange look. "But you can't plan everything in life, you know."

I disagree. In my experience, you can plan for everything, as long as you make concise, detailed notes.

As I squeeze out some shower gel from the bottle, I run through my schedule out loud:

"Finish showering. Get dressed. Do hair and make-up. Brush Rosy's hair. Attach bow tie to her collar. Eat a healthy and nutritious breakfast. Give Rosy her breakfast. Brush teeth. Brush Rosy's teeth. Appearance check by Mum and Gabrielle.

"Leave Rosy in the care of Beth (Gabrielle's recommended PA for me). Be picked up by our driver for today, Hal, in a black Jaguar XJ Sentinel, to go to Buckingham Palace for an appointment with the Queen. Meet the Queen. Answer the Queen's questions intelligently and with grace.

"Be escorted out the room so that Mum can have a private audience with the Queen. Wait outside the room while Mum is formally asked to form a government and take the role of Prime Minister. Say goodbye to the Queen.

"Be taken from Buckingham Palace to 10 Downing Street by Hal in the black Jaguar XJ Sentinel. Practise wave in the car.

"Get out the car at 10 Downing Street and wave to

crowds. Stand next to Mum looking inspired while she gives an inspiring speech outside 10 Downing Street.

"Go in the front door. Greet the staff. Greet Rosy and Beth, who will already be there. Wait for the staff to fuss Rosy, which will likely take several minutes because she's the cutest dog in the world. Mum will be taken into the Cabinet Room to be briefed so she can begin choosing her Cabinet. Rosy and I will be shown around some of the private living quarters of what will soon be our new home. *10 Downing Street.*

"Whoa."

Squealing in excitement, I turn the water off and reach for my towel, before skipping back to my room, where Rosy is busy tearing a magazine to shreds.

It's time to get ready for the most important day of my life.

"So, are you and the Queen best friends now?"

Mum smiles, looking out the window as we drive through central London. Her bodyguard, Maya, stifles a laugh in the front seat.

"I don't think I can quite claim to be her best friend, but the meeting went very well."

I nod, getting my phone out of my bag. "I think she liked me."

"Of course she liked you. She was very impressed by you."

I sit up a little taller in my seat. "I hope so. I can't believe we were just at Buckingham Palace meeting the Queen. It's MAD!"

"I know." Mum glances down at her hands in her lap. "Very surreal."

"You've had a lot of support from celebrities," I tell her, scrolling through the news on my phone. "Hollywood actors, athletes, presenters, musicians. Everyone's talking about it. Even Naomi Starr has tweeted about you!"

"Who?"

I look at her like she's mad. "*Naomi Starr?* The singer? Honestly, Mum, she's the biggest popstar on the planet. Even *I* know that, and you know I'm not very good with pop music. Now that you're Prime Minister, you should really know these things."

She chuckles. "I should. What did she say?"

"That she fully supports you and is delighted that you'll be the first black female Prime Minister of the UK. She can't wait to see what you're going to achieve over the next few years."

Mum exhales. "Wow."

"Cool, right?"

"Yes. A lot of pressure on my shoulders," Mum says, looking out the window again.

"You can handle it. You can handle anything. Hey, maybe we should invite Naomi Starr to Downing Street! She could come for dinner! Then I could meet her and maybe we could be friends," I say wistfully, screenshotting her tweet so I can save it for ever.

"Maybe, although I don't think popstars are going to be very high up on the list of people to host at Downing Street. *But –*" she adds on seeing my disappointed expression – "I'm sure there will be something we can invite her to."

"Good." I nod firmly, slipping my phone back into my bag. "I can always organize it if you don't have time. I guess you'll be busy the next few days."

"Try the next few years."

"Right." I smile up at her. "Are you nervous?"

"Terrified. Do I look it?"

"No," I assure her. "You look ready to take charge and lead the way to a better Britain."

She laughs, her shoulders relaxing. "Did Gabrielle tell you to say that?"

"No! That was all me. Did it sound good?"

"It sounded *great*. Maybe you should do the speech instead," Mum says, looking a little more nervous as Hal

13

slows down and we see the huge crowd of photographers and supporters waiting.

They go wild when they see our car approaching. It seems like there are hundreds of people lining the pavement behind the police barriers all the way up the road. I gulp.

"Nah, I think you better stick to doing the speech, Mum." I turn away from the window to look her in the eye. "You've got this. Right?"

She smiles at me gratefully and reaches over to give my hand a squeeze.

"*We've* got this," she says determinedly.

It's official. I have the best mum in the world.

As the car pulls up to the kerb and the camera flashes start going off like crazy, I smooth down my dress and check my hair, which is pulled back into a neat high bun.

"Here we are. 10 Downing Street," Hal says, catching my eye in the rear-view mirror and flashing me a grin. "Welcome home."

CHAPTER TWO

Mum pauses. She looks directly at her audience, no need to glance down at the pages resting on the lectern in front of her. She knows her speech off by heart. So far she's delivered it perfectly. But she lets the silence linger a little bit longer, making sure that this final paragraph hits home.

Like everyone else in the country watching her very first speech as Prime Minister, I gaze at her in awe.

"We have a lot of work to do. There will be challenges along the way, for all of us. The right path is not necessarily the easiest. But when we come together, as a nation and community, we can achieve everything we set out to do. And we can achieve it with courage, integrity and kindness, holding fast to the values that our history has taught us to cherish and protect. I believe that. This government believes that. And now it's time to get to work. Thank you."

There's an eruption of cheers and applause as Mum finishes her speech and turns to me. Beaming at her, I move to her side and together we walk from the lectern to the front step of Number 10, stopping to turn and wave at the mass of people cheering her on.

The door opens and, with a quick glance at one another as if neither of us can quite believe this is happening, we take our first steps into 10 Downing Street. The staff have lined up to greet us, clapping at Mum's entrance. As Gabrielle readies herself to introduce us to everyone in the house, I have a moment to take in how beautiful this place is – there is a red carpet right down the middle of the hall, like we're heading into a posh movie premiere, a sparkling chandelier hanging above us from the amazingly high ceiling, old paintings in heavy gold frames on the walls and a huge china vase on the mantelpiece to the left, bursting with fresh cut roses.

"*Wow,*" I say under my breath.

How on earth am I ever going to feel at home here?

I already feel like I can't touch ANYTHING.

Which reminds me. Where is—

"ROSY!"

I've just been introduced to Tony, the housekeeper,

16

when I hear Beth's cry echo through the house. Rosy comes bursting in through some doors at the other end of the hall, barking excitedly, stopping in her tracks to look in our direction and see what's going on.

She must have just been out in the garden because she is COVERED in mud.

She spots me.

Uh-oh.

"Rosy! Stop!" Beth cries out, to no avail.

Running at full pelt, Rosy comes hurling down the hallway towards us, her ears flying up in the air, her slobbery tongue lolling from her jaws. She leaves a trail of wet, muddy paw prints down the pristine red carpet and specks of dirt come flying from her coat, splattering the walls and the legs of anyone she passes.

Forgetting to brake in time, she crashes into my legs and jumps up madly at me, leaving dark mud stains all down my dress. Her tail is wagging furiously, slapping Tony's suit trousers with dirt streaks.

Mum closes her eyes in exasperation. Tony simply takes a calm step backwards, so that his legs are no longer in range of Rosy's tail.

"Nice to meet you, Pearl," he says, continuing our introduction and seemingly unfazed by the chaos we've just experienced. "And this –" he looks down at my dog with a warm smile – "must be Rosy. I've always liked a dog with spirit."

And just like that, I felt right at home.

"PEARL ROSE FRANCIS!"

I wince at Mum's use of my full name. She only does that when she's really cross.

"Maybe I'll pretend I didn't hear that," I whisper to Tony.

He puts down his cup of tea and gives me a stern look. I've only been living in Downing Street for a week and I've already got used to Tony's stern looks.

"I don't think you should ignore your mother," he warns.

"PEARL ROSE FRANCIS, COME HERE NOW."

Tony leans back in his chair, raising his eyebrows at me. I've had a morning of history and science lessons with my personal tutors, and had sneaked into the kitchen to snaffle some biscuits during my break. It turns out it's Tony's break time too, so we were having a nice chat while he drank his tea and I had some Jammie Dodgers.

Everyone who works here is nice and they've been welcoming, but Tony is my favourite. He's very calm and knowledgeable, and he lets me steal sweets from the Cabinet Room when no one's looking. I don't know why anyone thinks that ministers need bowls of sweets and mints while they have all these important meetings, but apparently they're essential.

I suggested to Tony and Mum that it was also surely essential to put a daily bowl of sweets in the office where I have my school lessons.

And let me tell you, it hasn't gone unnoticed that my suggestion has been rudely ignored.

I feel very grateful that Mum agreed to let me try home-schooling if she was made Prime Minister. I've never fit in at school. I feel like I always say the wrong thing or don't have the right look to make friends. I tried to be like them, but that didn't work, so in the end I decided it best to go under the radar at school, keeping my head down without bothering anyone. During Mum's campaign, I thought people might start liking me because they'd be impressed, but it was the opposite. I wasn't invisible any more and when one of the worst bullies in the year above saw a picture of me in the papers wearing a pink blouse with all these pretty bows on it, he laughed and called me "Prissy Pearl". The name stuck.

Thankfully, I now don't have to put up with him or any other idiots. I have peaceful, studious lessons every day with a variety of brilliant tutors. And none of them call me names.

"What did Rosy do now?" Tony asks, as Mum's furious voice echoes round the house again and I reluctantly stand up from the table.

"How do you know it's something to do with Rosy?" I say defensively.

I receive one of those famous looks again.

The thing is, Rosy is taking a *little* more time than everyone else to adjust to her new surroundings. It's not easy for a dog to move house, so it's natural for her to find things a bit disconcerting, but I was hoping she'd slip into her new routine more smoothly than she has. So far, not one day has passed without Rosy causing some kind of chaos, sometimes on a level of national importance.

For example, on Friday when she suddenly jumped up on the lap of the Chancellor of the Exchequer, giving her such a fright that she knocked over her coffee and it splashed over important budget papers.

Or last Wednesday, when Rosy discovered the fun new game of taking a run up and then sliding across the shiny black-and-white chequered tiles in the entrance hall, tumbling each time into the ankles of the custodian, the man whose job it is to open and close the front door.

On the fourth time she did it, he threatened to shut her out for good.

I *think* he was joking.

And she didn't make things better for herself when she almost pulled Mum to the ground in front of the paparazzi on her Saturday walk. She saw a squirrel and went for it.

"You see this?" Mum said the next morning, sliding the Sunday newspapers over the table at breakfast.

Every day at 6 a.m., Mum is given a full briefing of everything said in the papers so she's fully informed. But that day, just one glance at the headlines was enough. They all had the same picture on the front page of the exact moment Rosy spotted the squirrel, her eyes bright and alert, her big ears flying up as she bolted across the grass, and Mum lurching forwards, desperately holding on to the lead with a surprised expression, her mouth in the form of a giant "O".

I looked at the headlines and grimaced.

HAVE A NICE TRIP, PRIME MINISTER!

Patrice Francis narrowly avoids an embarrassing fall.

PM TAKES THE LEAD?

Our new Prime Minister can't control her dog! Can she keep control of our nation?

PATRICE LETS THE DOG OUT!

What the Prime Minister's spoilt, pampered pup says about her leadership ability.

"I think you look *great*," I said as chirpily as I could muster. "Really. I mean it. Your hair in this picture is really ... um ... on point."

She narrowed her eyes at me.

"I've been in this job for just one month. If Rosy does anything more to embarrass—"

"She won't," I said confidently. "I promise. I'll do some training with her every evening. You won't even notice she's here."

A few hours later, I drew up the perfect dog-training plan based on various YouTube tutorials and magazine articles. Unfortunately, Rosy isn't exactly a fast learner and seems to get distracted very easily. And I don't get as much time to spend on her training as I'd like. I had scheduled in an hour with her yesterday, but in the end only got ten minutes, what with a full day of tutoring, homework, a piano lesson followed by piano practice, and then dinner with the Prime Minister of France.

"PEARL!" Mum wouldn't normally yell like this for

me, but she must have checked in with my tutor and seen I wasn't there.

"Tony, any chance you need me right now for a very important job?" I plead. "Something that absolutely can't wait? Something that means I have to talk to Mum about this later?"

He chuckles. "Afraid not, Pearl. Looks like you have to face the music."

"Traitor."

"Coward."

I stick my tongue out at him. Not a particularly eloquent comeback but all I could come up with under pressure.

As Tony gives me an encouraging salute, I open the door of the kitchen and sidle into the hall where Mum is waiting for me with Rosy tucked under her arm. Mum's expression is thunderous. Next to her is her adviser Sebastian, now officially appointed the First Secretary of State, who looks very solemn.

Sebastian *always* looks solemn. I don't think I've ever seen him smile.

"Oh hey, Mum!" I say breezily, approaching them. "Did you call?"

"Yes," she replies furiously. "I did."

"Hi, Sebastian! Excellent tie. And Maya, hey!" While

23

Sebastian and Mum share a look, I wave at Mum's bodyguard who is standing a couple of steps behind her. "How are you? You look great! New suit? How's your morning going?"

The corners of Maya's mouth twitch as she tries to suppress a smile. Mum rolls her eyes.

"Oh no, you don't," she says, wagging her finger at me. "You are not getting out of this conversation, so don't try your distraction methods."

"I don't know what you're talking about," I say innocently, straightening the collar of my blouse. "By the way, nice job on the pledge of action for mental health this morning, I thought the press release was really well-constructed and I—"

"It won't work, Pearl," Mum interrupts, lifting her free hand to signal I stop talking. "You're not getting out of this one. Rosy just barrelled into the Cabinet Room."

"Did she? Huh. Strange, she doesn't usually—"

"We were in the middle of a very important meeting," Sebastian grumbles.

"Someone must have left the door open, because she's never—"

"*She jumped up on to the table*," Mum seethes.

"Wow! You have to admit, that's kind of impressive. She's very agile."

"It was absolute CHAOS!" Mum declares, handing Rosy over to me as she starts to scrabble about, trying to get down. "We tried catching her but she kept slipping through people's hands, running up and down the table, sending papers and files flying across the room, barking away as though it was some sort of game!"

"Now, Mum, remember it's never the dog's fault," I say calmly, letting Rosy lick my face as I give her a tickle under the chin. "It's the owner's fault. Clearly you didn't use the firm tone I told you about."

Mum's eyes bulge out of her head, her nostrils flare and her fists clench. Maya shifts uncomfortably behind her and gives me a look that says, "ABORT, ABORT."

Whoops.

I *may* have made things worse.

"Pearl Rose Francis, are you saying it was MY FAULT that YOUR dog burst into an IMPORTANT CABINET MEETING and RUINED IT?" Mum cries, throwing her hands up in exasperation. "The Secretary of State for Defence attempted to throw his arms around her as she hurtled past him and in doing so, he knocked over his glass of water and it went all over his suit, and now it looks like ... well, it looks like he wet himself!"

I purse my lips, desperately trying not to laugh. "Oh no."

"Oh no indeed," Mum says, giving me a warning look as I let out an accidental snigger. "Pearl, you HAVE to do something. You were the one who begged me to get a dog. Rosy is your responsibility. This misbehaviour can't go on. Do you understand?"

Rosy and I look at each other as she sits cradled in my arms.

"I understand," I sigh, holding her close. "I'll look into hiring a trainer as soon as possible."

"Good. I want a list of suggestions by tonight."

I nod. The door to the toilets swings open and the Secretary of State for Defence comes out, rubbing his trousers frantically with paper towels, muttering to himself. He glances up and sees us, clearing his throat.

"Sorry again about that, Justin," Mum says, looking pained. "Please do send me the dry-cleaning bill."

"Not to worry, Prime Minister," he replies, eyeing Rosy warily. "It's only water."

"Sorry, Justin," I mumble, dropping my eyes to the floor as he passes.

He goes back into the Cabinet Room and there's a distinct roar of laughter. The door shuts behind him and we fall back into silence, Mum closing her eyes in despair.

"You know," I begin, attempting to lighten the

atmosphere, "I think, if anything, the water was a great improvement on those trousers. That light grey doesn't really suit him, whereas the dark grey patch looked very good."

Mum exhales loudly. "A list of suitable dog trainers *by tonight*."

With that, she turns on her heel and marches back to the Cabinet Room with Maya and Sebastian in tow, the door slamming firmly behind them.

CHAPTER THREE

"I declare this children's hospital wing . . . OPEN!"

The crowd cheers and claps as I cut the purple ribbon with an unusually large pair of scissors. Smiling at my audience, I take a moment to pose for the photographers next to the Chief Executive Officer of the hospital, a very nice woman named Fiona.

"Thank you so much," she says, gesturing for me to follow her into the building so she can show me round the facilities. "It's such an honour to have you here."

"It's an honour for me to be invited," I reply, clasping my hands behind my back. "Tell me about these wonderful paintings on the wall here. Were they competition winners?"

As Fiona launches into a detailed explanation about the colourful artwork, I listen intently, keeping eye contact and asking specific, thoughtful questions, although being careful not to interrupt. One of the most amazing things about watching my mum interact with people is how she makes everyone feel incredibly important to her. They feel that she's listening to every word they say, because she is, and I want to make sure that I do the same.

If I'm going to be Prime Minister one day too, which I plan to, I need every bit of advice I can get.

"Such a small, easy thing to listen to someone," Mum's told me before. "But you'd be surprised how few people do it. How can you believe that you have something important to say if you don't think anyone is really listening?"

I've kept this in mind during all my recent public events and, according to Beth – now officially my assistant – the feedback has been extremely positive. I made sure she told Mum and urged her to exaggerate. I'm still making up for Rosy's behaviour.

I did just as Mum asked and researched lots of dog trainers, but it's difficult to find someone who ticks all the boxes. They need to be available to start straight away, which means dropping all their other clients, AND they need to be trustworthy and discreet. We don't want anyone who will spill things to the press. Beth and I have already held three interviews for the position and not ONE of them went well.

In fact, they went terribly, as anyone can see from my beautifully presented notes:

TRAINER NUMBER ONE
Name: GERI WHISTLER
Company: POW WOW POOCH TRAINERS
Qualifications: Principles of Dog Training and
Behaviour Qualification (Distinction); Kennel Club
Accredited; Diploma in Canine Behaviour

- Excellent first impression. Firm handshake. Warm smile. Promising.
- Booming voice. Might be too booming.
- DEFINITELY too booming.
- A secret service agent just came running in to see what the booming was.
- How is she getting LOUDER?!
- Rosy has run away to hide from the booming.

Conclusion: No.
Follow-up notes: Get eardrums tested.

TRAINER NUMBER TWO
Name: LUCAS HAY
Company: PAWESOME PALS

Qualifications: First Class Honours in Applied Animal Behaviour; Clinical Animal Behaviourist

- First impression: Clearly has an interesting taste in hats.
- Method: Engage Rosy in soothing performance art.
- Rosy not engaged thus far, but I remain hopeful.
- Uh-oh.
- Rosy has stolen his hat.
- Rosy not giving up hat.
- He's chasing Rosy around the room.
- Rosy is having the time of her life.
- Lucas is not.

Conclusion: No.
Follow-up notes: Buy Lucas a new hat.

TRAINER NUMBER THREE
Name: JULES JEFFERSON
Company: GET ON PUP!
Qualifications: PETbc Diploma in Canine Behaviour and Psychology; Diploma in Canine Anatomy and Physiology

- First impression: Smartly dressed, giving off a firm but fair vibe.

- Perhaps will be a modern-day Mary Poppins.
- OK, I was wrong.
- She is not firm at all.
- She is talking to Rosy like she's a baby.
- Rosy looks disturbed.
- Jules has pulled a tutu out of her bag.
- Why has she got a tutu in her bag?
- Oh. She wants to put Rosy in the tutu.
- Rosy has torn up the tutu.
- Jules is very upset.
- She made the tutu herself.

Conclusion: No.
Follow-up notes: Never attempt to dress Rosy.

They were all a complete DISASTER. I don't know what I'm going to do. Beth has promised to help me research other trainers this evening, once we're finished for the day, but I'm not sure how we're going to fit it in. After my tour of the new hospital wing, I have to go to the Everyday Hero Awards where I'm presenting the Teen Hero trophy, followed by a black-tie dinner with the Spanish Ambassador. I suppose I can research trainers in bed, but I need an early night, what with the fashion exhibition I'm opening tomorrow morning before lessons.

"Thank you again so much for your support, Pearl, I can't tell you how much it means," Fiona says, leading me out to the hospital carpark where my car is waiting. "I'm a huge fan of your mum. We all cheered here when she was elected."

"Me too," I say, making her chuckle. "Thank you for having me, and I look forward to hearing an update from you soon."

Waving one last time at the photographers, I slide into the backseat of the car followed by Beth, who is on the phone to someone from Battersea Dogs & Cats Home, confirming my appearance there next weekend. She shuts the door behind her and the driver sets off, heading into central London for the awards.

"I have someone bringing your dress and shoes for the dinner tonight to the hotel where the awards are being presented," Beth informs me as she finishes her call and sits back. "The hotel is giving you a room to use when the awards finish, so you can get ready in there. It means we'll get to the black-tie event on time."

"Perfect," I say with a nod, grabbing a bottle of water from the refrigerated compartment. "I think that went very well, don't you?"

"You were great, they loved you," Beth confirms, checking something on her iPad.

"I need to put a reminder in my diary to make sure I contact Fiona in a couple of weeks to check in. I want to make sure she knows I'm committed to hearing about the hospital's progress."

"Of course." Beth smiles. "I'll add it in now."

"Thank you. Oh, did you call that teacher from the performing arts school who got in touch? We could fit in a meeting with him on Thursday evening. I think I have a brunch meeting with an environmental charity that day, and a string recital in the afternoon. I can meet with him after my piano lesson, before dinner."

Beth hesitates. "I haven't got back to him yet, but I will. I actually wanted to hold off on scheduling that in for a couple of weeks."

"Why?"

"I wondered whether you've got a bit too much on," she says carefully, glancing at my schedule up on her screen, every square filled with colour-coordinated plans. "I wanted to make sure you had some time off. You know, to have fun."

"I have plenty of fun time off," I say, surprised. "Tonight, for example."

"The black-tie dinner with the Spanish Ambassador?"

"Right."

She nods slowly. "Technically, though, that's work.

I'm talking about time off to do stuff that teenagers should be doing. Like, hang out with your friends, watch a film, learn a dance or something." She shrugs.

I blink at her. "Learn a dance? You mean, like the waltz? Or the rumba? I was actually taught a few steps of the cha-cha-cha by one of the *Strictly Come Dancing* winners at an event for Mum a few months ago. It's very technical, but I think I got the hang of it."

"No." She giggles. "I mean, blare some loud music in your bedroom and make up a silly routine together. I have a niece your age and she loves doing that. She and her friends put on performances for us."

"Oh." I look down at my hands. "That does sound fun."

"I'm worried about you running out of steam," Beth says, smiling gently at me. "Remember, it's your mum who's Prime Minister. Not you. So, how about I leave Thursday evening free so you can do whatever you want."

"Thanks, Beth, but all my friends have a busy week, so you can go ahead and schedule that meeting in," I say cheerily. "But thank you for being so considerate."

She nods and turns her attention back to the iPad. I look out the window, pretending to be distracted by the beautiful city sights we're passing. But I barely notice them. I'm thinking about what Beth suggested, trying not to give away how I'm really feeling.

I would love to spend Thursday evening blaring music from my room and making up a silly dance. I'd love to invite my friends over. But there's just one problem.

I don't have any.

"And here to present the award for Britain's Animal Hero of the Year is world-renowned dog trainer, Jackson Williams!"

What did the announcer just say?

"Beth," I say, leaning over to whisper in her ear as a tall, confident man with thick dark hair marches on to the stage to great applause. "Who is that guy?"

"Jackson Williams!" She looks mildly surprised that I've had to ask. "Haven't you seen his TV show? It's amazing. He goes around the country training untrainable dogs, including those in rescue centres that can't be rehomed. By the end of the show, they've always found a new family. He takes on any challenge, no dog left behind. He's so . . . *dreamy.*"

I wrinkle my nose in disgust at the wistful expression on her face as she stares up at him, clapping much too enthusiastically.

"Thank you so much for having me here today," he

says into the microphone, beaming at the audience. "I couldn't be happier to be presenting this award to an animal who has shown incredible bravery, loyalty and intelligence."

As he continues his speech and reads out the nominees, I lean back towards Beth. "Did you say he trains *untrainable* dogs?"

She nods. "He's the best."

"Beth, I'm going to need you to go talk to him after the ceremony."

Her eyes light up with excitement. "*Really?*"

"Really," I confirm, a smile spreading across my face as he announces the winner – a police dog named Squid, who's saved hundreds of lives. "Tell him that, if he's interested, we've got an exciting new challenge for him."

CHAPTER FOUR

"*Jackson Williams?*" Mum frowns at me. "Are you serious?"

I have to admit this wasn't the reaction I was expecting when I came into her office to tell her the good news. I thought that she'd be over the moon that I had not only found the perfect trainer to sort out Rosy's issues, but that he also happened to be a bit of a celebrity, so he wasn't fazed in the slightest about taking on the dog of the Prime Minister.

When I spoke to him after the show, he was very intrigued about the job and asked me loads of questions, not just about Rosy but about Mum, too. He said he'd be happy to come meet Rosy and check they were the right fit, but that I had to make sure Mum was completely OK with it.

"Of course she'll be OK with it!" I exclaimed, as Beth

fluttered her eyelashes at him and fanned herself with her iPad.

I have to say, for an old person, he is quite handsome, so I guess I can understand why Beth was acting so strange around him. He was very nice, too, warm and approachable. Sometimes you can tell when a person has a gentle aura as soon as you meet them. He's one of those people.

Tony says I have the aura of a determined bull.

I take that to be a compliment.

"Mum, I am completely serious," I tell her now as she looks at me in disbelief. "He'll be here in half an hour. You've heard of him then?"

"Yeah," she says, nodding slowly. "I've heard of him."

"Apparently he has his own TV show and can train any dog," I say proudly, folding my arms. "Rosy will be in very good hands. I have a lot of hope for this one, especially after those disastrous interviews. He's come to the end of filming for the new season, which is perfect timing because now he can commit to Rosy for a few months at least. It's like fate! He's very nice, Mum, you'll like him a lot."

"Hang on," she says, standing up and pacing around the office. "You told Jackson Williams that you wanted him to be your dog trainer. And he . . . he said yes?"

"Exactly."

"And he knew who you were?"

I put my hands on my hips. "Yes, he knew who I was."

"He knew you were my daughter."

"Yeeees?" I blink at her. "Mum, what's going on? Why are you being weird?"

She opens her mouth to answer, but there's a sharp knock at the door and Sebastian comes barrelling in, all self-important and irritated.

"Sorry to disturb, Prime Minister," he says, before scowling at me. "What are you doing in here *during office hours?*"

I know that Sebastian is a brilliant politician and he's Mum's closest confidant and everything, but he's also . . . well. . .

SUCH a miserable grump.

Firstly, he always talks down to me, like I'm a child. And yes, OK, I realize that I am a teenager, but I'm a very mature one. Everyone says so.

Secondly, he doesn't even TRY to be nice to me. You'd think he'd at least pretend in the name of politeness, but apparently Sebastian doesn't care about manners. He's openly dismissive of me. I've spoken to Mum about this and she always chuckles and says something along the lines of, "He's not good with children, Pearl, but he's a brilliant and kind man. You should respect him."

Well, I'm sorry, but I find it very hard to respect someone who just a few days ago asked if a lunch box that was in the Downing Street Lost and Found belonged to me.

It had Peppa Pig on it.

"Hello, Sebastian," I say, standing as tall as possible. "I made an appointment via Gabrielle to have five minutes with Mum. What are *you* doing here?"

"Pearl," Mum says in a warning tone.

"I have some important things to go through with you, Prime Minister," Sebastian says, talking over me. "They can't wait."

I roll my eyes. "Fine. Mum, is that a yes to Jackson Williams then? If he connects with Rosy, you're happy for me to hire him?"

"I . . . uh . . . I –" she rubs her forehead – "all right."

"Great. Thanks, Mum," I say, heading to the door.

"Yes. Right," she says, distracted.

"See you, Sebastian," I mutter.

"Goodbye, Pearl," he grumbles.

I close her office door, high-five Maya who is guarding it, and head down the corridor to where Beth is waiting, busily typing something into her phone. She looks up at me hopefully.

"What did she say?"

"She said she thinks it's a brilliant idea!" I exclaim. "She's happy for us to hire him if he passes our test."

"Oh my goodness, then he'd be here every day!" Beth swoons at the idea. "He'll arrive any minute. Let's go get Rosy."

I follow her up the stairs to my room, nodding enthusiastically as Beth rambles on about the amazing Jackson Williams, but unable to shake my confusion over Mum's reaction. She was acting so weird just now.

I have a feeling there's something she's not telling me.

"You DATED?" My mouth falls open and Rosy barks for no reason at all. "*Mum!*"

"I know, I know, I should have told you," she says, burying her head in her hands.

She's sitting on the edge of my bed, having come in to say goodnight to me and Rosy, and also drop this huge bombshell on us. The reason Mum behaved so strangely when I mentioned Jackson Williams? Oh, it turns out that they used to be AN ITEM. As in, boyfriend and girlfriend.

Gross.

"It was years ago," she says, looking at me apologetically. "We were childhood sweethearts. We went to school together."

"Jackson Williams? Are you sure?"

"Yes, I'm sure," she sighs. "We were very close growing up. We were together for a few years."

"Mum!" I say, as Rosy paws at me for attention. "I can't believe you didn't tell me this!"

"I was about to, but then Sebastian came in! And my day was too busy!"

"Oh, really? Your day was so hectic that you couldn't find one minute to take me to the side and be like, 'By the way, Pearl, I actually do know this guy'? Mum! I hired him!" I throw my hands up in the air. "I can't fire him before he's even started his first day!"

Mum looks surprised. "I'm not asking you to fire him."

"You don't think it's going to be weird?"

"It may be weird when I first see him after all these years, but then it will be fine I'm sure." She gulps. "We're both grown-ups."

I shake my head at her in disbelief. I've finally found someone perfect to train Rosy and now this. *What are the chances?* Mum hasn't dated in years, basically ever since my dad, and he left us when I was so little, I can't remember him. She's never mentioned any other boyfriends before. I didn't even realize there *was* anyone before my father. I guess I've never really thought about it.

"Did it end badly?" I ask, trying not to sound too annoyed. Technically, this isn't really Mum's fault. I should have done a full background check before I told Jackson he had the job. You see? This is why you NEVER rush into anything unprepared. This is EXACTLY what happens when you don't do thorough notes.

You end up accidentally hiring your mum's secret ex-boyfriend.

"No, it ended ... well, it just ended." She shrugs, fiddling with the corner of my duvet cover. "We went on different paths and it didn't make sense at the time. He was always lovely. So smart and funny and kind. Life ... got in the way."

"Oh no," I say, slumping back into my pillows.

"What?"

"You still *like* him."

"WHAT? No, I don't!" she says hurriedly, looking all flustered.

"Then why did you just get that dreamy look in your eye when you were talking about him?"

"I did NOT get a dreamy look in my eye!"

"Yes, you did."

"Pearl!" Her voice sounds strained. "No, I did not. Look, this isn't a big deal. It was a long time ago and I thought you should know. In case he says anything about me." She pauses. "Did he?"

"Did he what?"

"Say anything about me."

"He said he thinks you're very beautiful and he still loves you."

"He *what*?" she gasps, her eyes widening. "Really?"

"NO! That was a TEST."

"Pearl!"

She leans forward to grab the spare pillow, hitting me with it and making me laugh. Rosy jumps at the pillow and attacks it – she loves this game.

"Mum, seriously though. Is it going to be a problem? We can get someone else."

"No. I'm glad you found someone who can handle this mischievous pup," she says, desperately trying to get Rosy to release the pillow from her jaws. "It will be fine."

"OK. Good. You won't even have to see him that much. You'll be busy, you know, running the country."

"Exactly," she says, giving up and letting Rosy take the pillow to the other side of the bed to destroy. She checks her watch and lets out a long sigh. "I'd better get back to it. Sebastian is waiting downstairs. He's in a bad mood today."

I frown. "He's always in a bad mood."

"Maybe that has something to do with Rosy chewing his umbrella."

"She didn't know it was *his* umbrella," I argue, watching Rosy fondly as she tears open the pillowcase. "She picked one from the stand by the door. It could have been anyone's."

"Night, Pearl," Mum says wearily.

"Night, Mum."

She kisses my head before leaving the room. As soon as she's gone, I turn to Rosy, who looks up at me, busily chewing on pillow fluff. I grin at her.

"Night, Rosy," I say, reaching to turn off my bedside lamp. "And good going on Sebastian's umbrella."

CHAPTER FIVE

It turns out that the hype about Jackson Williams is all true.

Just a few weeks with him and Rosy is the most beautifully behaved Cocker Spaniel in the world. The change in her is AMAZING. She knows all the commands: she sits when you tell her to, she comes when you call her name and she doesn't eat her food until you give her the go-ahead. All the staff at Downing Street love her now, and she hasn't barged in on any meetings or ruined anyone's things, or caused Mum any embarrassment. She has her morning training session with Jackson and then the rest of the day, she happily sits next to me while I have my lessons or, if she can, she accompanies me to whatever event I need to go to. She's even more perfect than she already was.

Jackson says it's all about patience and establishing authority.

But I think it's more like he's some kind of magician.

I thought it would take him YEARS to whip Rosy into shape. The other day I heard the door custodian say proudly to a visitor, "Oh yes, that's little Rosy. The Downing Street Dog."

The Downing Street Dog! This was said by the man who once asked Mum if it was possible to pass a law banning dogs from the house!

I don't want to take the credit or anything, because of course it is all Jackson's work, but I have to say I'm very pleased that I was the one who went about hiring him. And it hasn't been weird between him and Mum at all. In fact, they've barely seen each other, so it turns out we didn't have anything to worry about.

Sure, the first day was a *bit* weird.

I've never seen Mum so *shy* before. She's usually super confident and intimidating, but with Jackson she went all quiet and awkward. He had already passed his trial with Rosy with flying colours and then, once all his background and security checks had been sorted, he'd been officially hired and started work the following Monday.

"Rosy, you remember Jackson," I said as Rosy

attacked his shoelaces out in the garden round the back of the house.

"Hello again, Rosy." He smiled, crouching down and tugging the shoelaces from her jaw. "I see we have lots of work to do."

"Shall I leave you to it?"

"Actually, Pearl, it would be very helpful if you could be in on as many training sessions as possible. As I mentioned in the interview, I train the owner as well as the dog."

"Right." I nodded. "No problem. I think I am a bit soft on her. Probably making her worse."

"Usually the way. And . . . uh . . . will I be seeing your mum at all? I appreciate she's busy. . ." He trailed off and I immediately felt the blood rising to my cheeks.

I hadn't told him I knew about their past yet and wasn't quite sure how to bring it up.

"She said she'd pop in at some point today; she wants to see you. You know, because of Rosy. She wants to see what you're like with Rosy." I cleared my throat and he shifted uncomfortably. "Anyway, shall we start?"

"Let's."

A few minutes later, Mum strolled out with Maya in tow, and Jackson instantly grew a few inches taller. I would have smirked, but I was too busy trying to get

Rosy to come back to me from where she was digging up a rose bush.

"Jackson. Hi," Mum said, smiling bashfully and tucking her hair behind her ear. Which was weird because I could have sworn that earlier she'd had her hair tied back.

"Prime Minister," he replied, shaking her hand.

"Come on, Jackson." She laughed. "You must know you can call me Patrice."

"It's great to see you again."

"It's great to see you."

There was an awkward pause.

"You've done very well," Mum blurted out. "Your TV show is so successful. Congratulations."

"I think if we're going to talk about the careers of everyone here, mine isn't the first that springs to mind," Jackson chuckled, and her eyes dropped modestly to the ground. "I always knew you were destined for great things. The first black female Prime Minister. Breaking barriers, making history. *You did it.*"

She smiled. "Thank you."

He smiled back, his eyes gleaming.

Honestly.

"Oh look! Rosy is doing a POOP," I said loudly, in order to bring a stop to this nonsense.

I appreciate it was a bit childish of me, but someone had to do something. I noticed Maya smirk at her shoes. Anyway, it worked. They both snapped out of their dreamy expressions and collected themselves.

"I had better get back to work," Mum said, pointing back at the house.

"Me too," Jackson said, gesturing to Rosy.

"Thank you for taking Rosy on. I'm sure you'll do a brilliant job."

"No problem. Thank *you* for all the work you're doing. Your country appreciates it," he said, jokingly punching the air with his fist.

"Haha, great, thank you," she said, before turning back to the house.

So, yes, that had been excruciating to witness.

But they'd had hardly any other contact since, just passed each other in the house a few times, and they acted much more professionally then. They barely acknowledged one another.

And just as Rosy has FINALLY settled into her new role as the Downing Street Dog, so Mum has smashed her first few months as Prime Minister. The public love her. According to Gabrielle, her approval ratings are very high. Mum told me a long time ago that as a black single mother, she was going to have to work even harder to get to where she wanted to be, and I'm so proud that she's doing so well, rising to every challenge that comes her way.

I think I'm doing OK as Britain's "First Daughter", too. Despite Beth's concerns about how little downtime I get, I actually like being really busy. I've already met some amazing people and gone to some incredible events, plus I have Rosy to keep me company at home.

The only downside is some of the things I read about me and Mum.

"When you're in the public eye, you're never going to please everyone," Mum says, when I see something mean about her in the papers or online. "When you're Prime Minister, receiving criticism is all part of the job. It's right that people question my decisions. The only thing I'm sorry about is you being involved in any of it."

It's rare that newspapers print bad things about me, but online it's different. I try not to look, but it's hard when you're tagged in posts. One point of contention seems to be the way I dress.

"Beth, do you think I have a sense of style?" I asked this morning, when we were in the car on the way back from a private showing of a new photography exhibition.

The subject of the exhibition was dogs, so I didn't hesitate to accept the invitation and I even got to bring

Rosy along. The photographers who were invited to get pictures of me looking at pictures – I know, it's strange when you think about it – all thought Rosy was adorable, and got some lovely snaps of me holding her up to inspect the dogs staring out at her from the picture frames.

"Of course you have a sense of style!" Beth replied, surprised at my question. "Why do you ask that?"

"Someone on Twitter said I didn't have one," I sighed, stroking Rosy's head. "Lots of people agreed."

"What have I told you about reading that nonsense? I hope you blocked whoever it was. People will always be jealous and spiteful, and social media is the perfect place for them to let it all out at a safe distance," Beth said crossly. "You shouldn't be looking at any of it."

I know she's right, and Mum's told me so many times to stay away from social media, but it's difficult not to take a peek now and then, just to see what people think of you. I try not to let it get to me and lots of people are very supportive, but every now and then a small comment like that can sting.

Maybe I need to ask Mum if I can borrow her stylist every now and then for some tips.

I can ask her about it tonight at dinner. It's going to be just us two. Mum tries to have mealtimes together as much as possible, but sometimes she can't, which I completely understand. I'm happy to eat with Rosy, and sometimes Beth will join me, which is nice.

But this afternoon when I was back from the exhibition, Mum interrupted my French lesson by popping her head round the door and saying that she'd told Beth to clear my schedule tonight for a special dinner.

"What's the occasion?" I asked.

"Nothing," she said. "Just ... dinner."

She was a bit flustered when she told me about it. I asked my French tutor if he thought she'd sounded strange, but he said he didn't notice anything unusual. Then he told me to stop looking so suspicious and focus on my grammar.

"What are you doing this evening?" I ask Beth once she's finished going through my schedule for tomorrow and I get ready to head to the dining room.

"My two nieces are coming over for a sleepover," she says, beaming at me as she puts on her coat. "Are you looking forward to a night with your mum? I bet Chef is whipping you up something delicious."

"Yes, I think we're having a starter of charred kale with citrus and green tahini, beetroot ravioli for main and then plum *clafoutis* for pudding."

She straightens the collar of her coat and gives me a quizzical look. "*Clafoutis*?"

"It's a baked French dessert. Kind of like a pie, I think."

"Wow! I'm jealous."

"What are you having at your sleepover?"

"We're ordering in pizzas to eat in front of a movie and then we're going to dig into tubs of ice cream." She grins, slinging her bag over her shoulder. "Not quite so glamorous as yours I'm afraid. I'll see you tomorrow morning, bright and early."

"See you tomorrow, Beth. Have a nice time with your nieces."

I wave her goodbye and then stroll through to the dining room, Rosy trotting at my heels. I took her for a long walk after my French lesson and she had a training session with Jackson this afternoon, so she's exhausted. She'll happily snooze on her bed while we eat – before Jackson came along, she'd whine and jump up at every mealtime, desperate to get the food off my plate. Occasionally, she'd succeed.

Pushing open the door to the dining room, I find it empty, with two places immaculately set out. I instruct Rosy to go to her bed in the corner, and then sit down at the table, fiddling with the cloth napkin and looking at the old paintings by famous artists while I wait for Mum. I am so lucky to live in this beautiful, historical house and have incredible dinners cooked for me.

But part of me would quite like to order pizza with friends and watch movies before digging into a tub of ice cream.

"Hi, Pearl, sorry I'm late," Mum says, bustling into the room with Sebastian. "Busy day."

I frown at Sebastian. "I thought we were having dinner just us two."

"We are," she assures me. "I need to sign some things and then I'm done. I didn't want you sitting in here much longer on your own."

"If you could sign here, Prime Minister," Sebastian says, ignoring me and putting some papers down on the table. "And this one, too."

"Perfect, thank you."

"Will you be able to join us in an hour?" he asks in a frustrated manner. "We wanted to go through some things with you about the conference next week. They can't wait."

"I'm spending tonight with my daughter, Sebastian," Mum reminds him, putting her hands on my shoulders.

He scowls. "I suppose *I* can sort it out, if you don't mind me taking charge."

"Of course. You can fill me in first thing tomorrow morning."

He nods and then leaves the room. Maya pops her

head round the door and lets us know she'll be outside. I notice she glares at Sebastian's back as he walks past and I smile to myself. She obviously likes him as much as I do.

"How was your day?" Mum asks, taking her seat and putting her napkin on her lap. "How was French?"

"Boring. We did grammar today."

"Grammar is always tricky," she says.

The door opens again as our food is brought in. I can't help but notice Mum is unusually fidgety. She's a very calm, collected person, but tonight she's fiddling with her cutlery and shifting in her chair.

"Are you OK?" I ask, picking up my fork to dig in.

"Yes! Yes, why wouldn't I be? Tell me more about your day," she says, hurriedly changing the subject.

"Not much to tell. Except, I've been thinking, could I borrow your stylist?"

"Why? What for?"

"I think I need some tips."

"Don't be ridiculous!"

"Please? I'm in the public eye too, Mum. I don't want to make any embarrassing or wrong decisions when it comes to my clothes."

"You should wear whatever you want to wear."

"Mum, I don't think you'd be happy if I wore my trousers on my head."

She looks amused, taking a sip of water. "Do you want to wear trousers on your head?"

"My point is, the fashion world is a minefield and it would be handy to have someone give me a little guidance so I don't make any kind of *faux pas* at a public event that might embarrass you or the government."

"I'll think about it." She smiles. "But if it means anything, I think you always look wonderful."

"Thanks. But you're my mum. You're a little bit biased."

We fall into comfortable silence, but after a while I notice that Mum isn't doing much eating. She's pushing her food round her plate, her forehead furrowed in concern. She often does this when she's got a big problem on her hands and she's working out how to solve it. It's like she can't switch off her brain.

"Pearl," she says eventually, putting her fork down as I finish eating, "there's something I need to talk to you about."

"Is everything OK?"

"Yes," she says with a nod, "everything's fine. I need to tell you something. I've been waiting for the right moment and, well, the right moment has been chosen for me." She pauses, taking a deep breath. "I've ... I've been seeing someone."

I blink at her. "Huh?"

"I've been dating someone."

My jaw drops to the floor. "You've been *dating*? How? When? How is this possible? You don't have time to date! And how have I not noticed?"

"We wanted to fly under the radar, it was such early days. I didn't want anyone knowing until I was certain it meant something. I definitely didn't want the press to find out. . ."

She trails off.

"The *press* has found out?" I ask carefully.

"Yes. That's why I'm telling you now. Gabrielle thinks the story is going to break in the morning. I've let him know so he's prepared, too."

"OK."

I try to let this all sink in but my brain is in a WHIRLWIND. Firstly, I can't believe my mum has been dating someone and I had no idea about it! Secondly, when could she have possibly found the time to go on dates? Where did they even go? Surely someone would have spotted them. How long have they been dating for? And who is this guy? How did they meet? Was it at a state dinner? Is he an ambassador or something important? Oh my god, is my mum dating someone ROYAL?

"Are you dating a prince?" I blurt out without thinking.

"What? No!" She gives me a strange look. "Why would you think that?"

"Well, you could be! I have too many questions and my brain is a jumble!"

"That's OK. You can ask me as many questions as you like," she says gently.

"First things first. Who is this person? Have I heard of them?"

"Yes, you have. You actually know them."

I gulp. Oh god.

Please don't let it be grumpy Sebastian. Please don't let it be grumpy Sebastian. . .

"All right then. Who is it?" I ask cautiously.

"It's Jackson." She smiles. "Jackson Williams."

CHAPTER SIX

IT'S LOVE AT NO.10!

Prime Minister spotted out and about with new partner, Jackson Williams!

DOGS, DATES AND DOWNING STREET...

Sources confirm Patrice Francis is in a relationship with her celebrity dog behaviourist.

PM'S SECRET LOVE AFFAIR!

How Patrice Francis fell in love with dishy dog trainer Jackson Williams!

OPINION PIECE: CAN SHE REALLY HAVE IT ALL?

Relationship Editor Cathy Cobb on how PM Patrice Francis will juggle leadership, family life AND a new relationship.

How did I not know about this?

Seriously, how have I been so blind? They've been dating this whole time, right under my nose, and I had NO IDEA.

I have to admit that there are some things that make a lot more sense now. Like how they barely acknowledged each other when they met around the house. I always thought it was a bit strange that they used to be so close and now pretended like the other one didn't really exist, even when in such close proximity.

Obviously now I know that they were ignoring each other on purpose to hide their secret connection.

GROSS.

And how I've noticed Mum putting on perfume before going to "important meetings" that happen to have been in the evening, but that no other ministers attended because they'd all gone home. Clearly, she wasn't going to meetings. She was going to dinner with Jackson.

SO SNEAKY.

Or how Mum has started singing in the shower. Recently she's been waking me up at 4.30 a.m., or whatever ridiculous hour she needs to be up and about, with her very out-of-tune vocals as she goes about her morning routine, which is something she's never done before. I put it down to the stress of the job or maybe a method of rallying herself in the morning before a big day. I didn't realize it was . . . *love*.

UGH!

How is this possible? I can't believe I didn't see this coming. I saw how they acted around each other that first day. I should have known this would happen. WHY WASN'T I PREPARED FOR THIS? There I was thinking that I had everything under control, all aspects of my life running smoothly, and it turns out this was going on the whole time!

I feel overwhelmed and very confused.

The thing is, Mum is so happy. I know that sounds cliché, but it's true. There's no denying that Jackson has brought out a change in her, what with all her singing and stuff.

At the same time, it's a lot for me to take in. Mum has a *boyfriend*. She's never had a boyfriend before. I don't really know how to handle the whole situation. I mean, technically there's no reason for me to be weird about it. I never knew my father and he never kept in touch, so it's not like I can be upset that Jackson might be replacing anybody. And Jackson is really nice and he loves Rosy, so in terms of a suitable partner for my mum, he ticks a lot of boxes.

But . . . but it's always been just me and Mum.

Plus, this has all been sprung on me very suddenly

and now EVERYBODY in the whole WORLD knows about it. The day Mum revealed her big secret to me, they were photographed holding hands on one of their secret dates – it's a grainy photo and taken from a distance, but it's definitely them. The world has gone mad over it. It's been a week since the story broke, and it's still the biggest headline in all the papers, even though there are much more important things going on in the world. Apparently my mum's love life is front page material.

Oh, and there's another small spanner in the works that Mum casually dropped into the conversation.

Jackson Williams has a daughter. Apparently, she's my age and also had no idea about any of this. When Mum was breaking the news to me over charred kale in Downing Street, Jackson was busy telling his daughter everything over pancakes in their North London home.

I don't know why Mum felt the need to give me the pancake detail, but there you go.

I can't remember reading about his daughter in all the research we did before taking him on as Rosy's trainer. I do know that he's a widower – his wife passed away five years ago – and I was aware he lived in London, but there were no other details about his personal life. He's notoriously private for someone with a television career. He never mentioned that he had a daughter my age in any of our training sessions.

Now, they want us *to meet*.

As if I don't have enough on my plate, trying to get my head round my mum dating our dog trainer behind my back, now I have to have dinner with him and his daughter and act like one big happy family.

"If you're not OK with it, just tell your mum," Beth suggests through the curtain of the changing room.

I asked her to come with me to Bond Street to pick the perfect outfit for this evening. I can't wear just anything. This is a BIG DEAL. Jackson is going to come to the front door of Number 10 with his daughter in tow, at dinner time, which means the press camped outside is going to know EXACTLY what's happening.

I have to find an outfit that says, *"You and your daughter are very welcome here, but if you hurt my mum I'm going to kill you."*

It's hard to pick a look that specific on your own.

"I *am* OK with it," I call back to Beth, doing up a zip on the side of a pink dress the shop owner picked out for me, one of many.

She also closed off the changing room area so no members of the public can come in.

"You don't sound OK with it. Maybe you need a bit more time to get used to the idea before having dinner

65

with him and his family."

"I'm not sure I'll ever get used to the idea," I sigh, before pulling the curtain back and stepping out.

Beth wrinkles her nose. "I think, for this occasion, that's a bit too..."

"Frilly?" I suggest, gesturing to the collar, sleeves and hem.

"Right. It's gorgeous. But too frilly for tonight."

I go back into the changing room and inspect my last two options, deciding to try the green pencil skirt with the white blouse next.

"Have you talked to your mum about your feelings?" she asks cautiously.

I step out of the dress and place it neatly back on its hanger.

"Sort of. Not exactly. It's hard to talk to her about it. She did ask if I felt it was too soon to meet Jackson's daughter, but she looked so excited at the idea. And it's only dinner, right?"

"Right. But I'm sure she wouldn't mind postponing until you feel more comfortable about everything."

I emerge from the changing room in the new outfit but can tell right away from Beth's expression that this isn't the one, so I walk back behind the curtain.

"One more to go," I call out to her. "We're running

out of options."

"We'll find something." She pauses. "I have a feeling you're going to get on well with Jackson's daughter. What's her name again?"

"Isabella."

"Isabella. Yes, you'll probably have lots in common," she says in an overly encouraging tone.

"Why do you think that? Because we're the same age?"

"You both love dogs. That's a good start."

"How do you know she loves dogs?" I pop my head round the curtain excitedly. "Did you research her and take notes?"

"No, Pearl," Beth says, rolling her eyes. "I did not research her."

"Oh." I continue with getting dressed. "Well, then, how do you know she likes dogs?"

"Her dad is a dog trainer! It would be difficult for her not to be a fan, right? So Rosy will be a perfect ice-breaker. I know the situation is difficult for you, but remember it's probably even stranger for her."

I step out in the final outfit. It's exactly what I was after: a pale blue knee-length dress with a smart matching jacket. Smart, bold and sophisticated.

"This is The One, right?"

"You look very grown-up."

"Perfect then." I hesitate, catching her eye in the mirror. "I suppose you may be right about everything being a lot trickier for Isabella. I can't imagine it's easy to get your head round your dad dating the Prime Minister when you've had no warning. I probably have to be the bigger person in this instance."

"Probably. It's going to be intimidating for her. No doubt she'll be nervous and shy, so go easy on her. I know it's a weird situation and it will be difficult for you—"

"Don't worry, I can handle anything," I assure her, smoothing down the lapels of the jacket and admiring my reflection in the mirror. I look just like the daughter of the Prime Minister should look. "I'm sure Isabella and I will get on very well."

Isabella Williams is the WORST and we will NEVER get on. Ever. Not in a million years.

I don't know what to do. I'm currently hiding in the toilet, hoping that when I come out, Jackson and his daughter will have somehow magically disappeared. I have never met someone so rude IN MY LIFE.

As soon as I set eyes on her, I should have known this was not going to go well.

We heard the noise from the paparazzi outside when

they arrived, shouting questions at Jackson, trying to get him to give a comment on his relationship with Mum. We were standing in the hall ready to greet our guests, the custodian opened the door and there was Jackson smiling on the doorstep. Next to him was a girl with curly, messy hair that looked as though it hadn't been brushed in a good few years, wearing a T-shirt with some band on it that I've never heard of and ripped black jeans.

RIPPED JEANS. FOR DINNER AT DOWNING STREET.

Of course, I didn't want to assume the worst straight away because you should never judge a book by its cover, so I plastered on a big smile and welcomed them both in, offering my hand for her to shake as I introduced myself. And do you know what she did? She looked at my outstretched hand and snorted.

Snorted! Like it's *stupid* to shake hands with someone when you first meet them! As though *I* was the one acting strangely.

I take my time checking my hair in the bathroom mirror, wondering how long I can get away with hiding in here. Honestly, what is with her? It's safe to say that neither of us wants to be in this situation, but at least I'm *pretending* to have an acceptable time! And as for Beth thinking Isabella would be all shy and intimidated, she couldn't have been more wrong! The minute she walked in, she seemed perfectly comfortable and confident, making it obvious to everyone that she was in a strop and had no intention of making an effort.

We may be the same age but our similarities end there. We could not be more different.

If I were to take notes on her, they would go something like this:

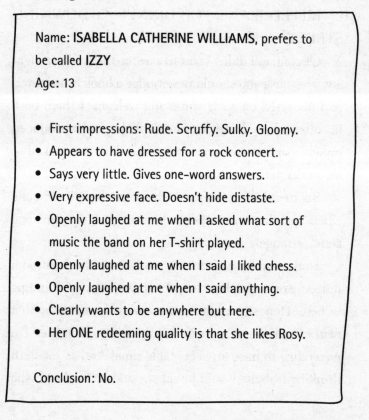

Name: **ISABELLA CATHERINE WILLIAMS**, prefers to be called **IZZY**

Age: 13

- First impressions: Rude. Scruffy. Sulky. Gloomy.
- Appears to have dressed for a rock concert.
- Says very little. Gives one-word answers.
- Very expressive face. Doesn't hide distaste.
- Openly laughed at me when I asked what sort of music the band on her T-shirt played.
- Openly laughed at me when I said I liked chess.
- Openly laughed at me when I said anything.
- Clearly wants to be anywhere but here.
- Her ONE redeeming quality is that she likes Rosy.

Conclusion: No.

(Follow-up notes: None. Although I have plenty of etiquette tips I could recommend her, should she ask.)

"Pearl?" There's a knock on the bathroom door. "Are you in there?"

I sigh. "Yes, Mum."

"Are you coming back to dinner or are you planning on locking yourself in the bathroom for the entire evening?"

"The latter."

"Come out please," she says in her sternest tone. "Don't make me ask Maya to break down the door."

I hear Maya go, "Ooh, very happy to do that, Ma'am!" and then Mum reply, "Thank you, Maya, that won't be necessary. But I'm rather startled at how eager you are to break down a door."

I reluctantly unlock the door and step out. "I was just sorting my hair."

"Your hair is always immaculate, Pearl. I know you were hiding in there," Mum says in a hushed tone, putting an arm around my shoulders and practically dragging me back to the dining room.

"She's *awful*," I whisper back. "Don't make me talk to her."

"Pearl," she warns. "These things take time. Get to know her."

71

"No thanks," I mutter under my breath, before entering the dining room with a polite smile on my face as though everything's fine.

Once we're seated and pudding has been served, the four of us fall into an uncomfortable silence and I notice Mum and Jackson giving each other eye signals across the table. Isabella doesn't spot their communication, she's too busy being unimpressed with her lemon tart and poking it with her fork.

"Why is this so ... yellow?" she asks, wrinkling her nose. "Is it meant to be yellow?"

"It's *lemon tart*," I say, narrowing my eyes at her.

She pushes her plate away. "I don't like stuff that has a slimy texture. Do you have any edible food?"

I purse my lips, looking at Mum wide-eyed, using all my willpower not to say, "*YOU SEE? This girl is a NIGHTMARE.*"

"Izzy, why don't you try it?" Jackson suggests through a fixed smile. "I think you'll like it if you give it a chance."

"No thanks." She looks at her watch. "Time to go home – right, Dad?"

"Actually –" he glances at Mum – "there's still something we'd like to discuss with you both."

I put my fork down and pat my lips with my napkin. I spot Isabella watching me and rolling her eyes.

OK, WHAT is wrong with using a NAPKIN?

Mum clears her throat. "Jackson and I have been talking, and we had an idea that we'd like to talk to you about. As you know, we've got very close the last couple of months—"

"—but really we've known each other for years," Jackson adds, smiling dreamily at Mum.

"Exactly." Mum smiles back. "Neither of us wants to waste any more time apart. We've already done enough of that."

"And considering I spend a lot of my time here anyway training Rosy and seeing Patrice, it seems a bit strange to keep going back and forth to our house," Jackson explains.

"So, we thought it made sense to take the next step. We want to see if we really can make this work. Long-term."

"Mum," I croak, dread seeping through my veins, "what exactly *is* the next step?"

She smiles at me hopefully. "We would like to live together."

"Izzy," Jackson says, taking her hand as her eyes widen in horror, "how would you feel about moving into 10 Downing Street?"

I read somewhere that writing down your feelings can help you to process them, so that's why I've decided to start this private blog...

(IF ANYONE IS READING THIS WHO ISN'T ME THEN GO AWAY!)

Anyway, yeah, I thought I'd start this because my handwriting is rubbish and I type faster, so a blog like this one made sense. I can get all my feelings out and maybe that way I'll feel a bit better.

So. My feelings right now.

Where shall I start? How about...

AHHHHHHHHHHHHHHHHRHGRGRGRGH GHRHRHRH!

I CANNOT believe my dad is doing this to me!! What is he THINKING? What have I done to deserve this?! One minute everything is fine, everything is good, and now suddenly it's all changing!!

First, he started dating without telling me, and not just anyone, the PRIME MINISTER, and now he wants us to MOVE IN with her and her horrible daughter!!

I feel like I'm living in a crazy nightmare, because this is all happening really fast. Why would he WANT to live there? Yeah that house is really nice and everything, but it's also a MUSEUM. It's so posh and fancy and there's photographers camped outside it all the time. Doesn't he want any privacy?!

I can't believe he's dating someone who's not Mum. Why does he feel the need to date ANYONE? Ever since Mum passed away five years ago, it's just been me and him. We've got our routine, we know how each other works, we've been coping OK.

And yes, I guess he's found it hard since Mum died, throwing himself into work just to keep busy so he doesn't have to think about how sad he is all the time with her gone. I don't mean to sound like a therapist or anything, I just understand how he feels because I feel the same. I miss her every day. All the time. And it sucks. So I know how it feels to want to keep busy.

But we were FINE. We did not need a stranger to come along and ruin everything.

I had a feeling something was going on the past few weeks. There was something different about him. He's been laughing more, even at things that aren't funny, which makes him look stupid. He hums happily while he does the washing-up, which is extremely annoying.

Who is happy doing the washing-up?! People in love, that's who.

So, I got suspicious and I had a feeling that maybe he'd met someone. Obviously I hated the idea of it. Mum is the love of his life. They loved each other more than anything. No one can replace her, no one should even try. So yeah, I thought to myself, *This sucks, but if he's met someone who makes him a bit happier than he has been, I can TRY to work towards being OK with it eventually.*

But I will NEVER be OK with HER. He could have dated anyone on the planet and he decides to go out with the PRIME MINISTER. How does he expect me to feel about this?! Since the news broke, our house has been surrounded by reporters, desperate to get a picture of him.

Because he's on TV, I'm used to getting a little bit of attention when I'm out with him; sometimes he gets recognized at the supermarket and stuff. But that is NOTHING compared to this. There are so many photographers and they shout questions at you, all speaking over each other so you can't hear a thing, and they shove cameras right in your way so walking suddenly becomes this hazard and you're terrified you're going to fall flat on your face.

So I decided I wasn't going to make this easy for him. I wasn't going to be on "my best behaviour" when I went to go meet her, like he asked me to.

Because he has chosen to ruin my life.

Look, I get that Patrice is an icon or whatever. HELLO, she's Patrice Francis! The first black female Prime Minister EVER. She's super intelligent and totally kick-ass, and basically an inspiration to everyone.

But I don't want to LIVE WITH HER. I don't want to live at 10 Downing Street and be photographed every day. I don't want to have to wear certain clothes and do certain things. I don't want her to act as though she's my MUM.

And more than anything, I don't want to live with her daughter.

Pearl Francis is EXACTLY how I imagined her to be. Stuck-up, cold and snobby. As soon as the door opened, I knew we weren't going to get on.

She acts and talks as though she's a hundred years old, and she dresses like it too. It's as though she's determined not to be a teenager, desperate not to lower herself to my level, like being our age is a bad thing.

We have ZERO in common. She doesn't like any

cool music, her hobbies are things like piano lessons (!) and chess (!!), and honestly, I think she might be under the impression that SHE'S the Prime Minister, not her mum. She's so prim and superior.

The moment we met, she looked down her nose at me.

I genuinely believe that she has never had a moment of fun in her life. And I'm expected to live with this person?

I hate this. It's not like I have a choice. I can't live by myself in our house. I have to live wherever Dad does, and he wants to live in Downing Street. I have to make sure that he knows how HORRIBLE this is for me, so he'll make up his own mind to pack up and go home to our house, just the two of us, where we belong.

I wish Mum were here so I could ask her what to do.

The ONLY good thing about this rubbish situation is the Downing Street Dog, Rosy. She's super cute. But whatever. If I have to share a room with snooty Pearl then I am going to LOSE IT.

We are never, ever going to be friends. EVER.

CHAPTER SEVEN

Oh. My. God. I have never been more embarrassed in my life.

I am going to kill her.

"Pearl, please let me in," Mum says, rapping her knuckles on my door for the billionth time. "It wasn't that bad."

"YES, IT WAS," I yell, pulling my duvet back over my head. "I am NEVER leaving my room AGAIN. And it's all because of HER!"

This is a slight exaggeration. The bit about it all being Izzy's fault is completely true, but I do intend to leave my room before the end of the day, purely because Rosy is in here with me and I need to let her out to go pee soon. Otherwise it would be cruel.

But if Rosy *wasn't* here, then I really would NEVER leave my room again.

Izzy has lived here for just a few days and in those few days, she has completely ruined my life. But this morning was the worst yet – I have been utterly humiliated. The most frustrating thing about it is, I thought we were making progress. She was being so nice to me today and I thought she was being genuine. I thought, *Hey, maybe she's not so bad after all*.

What. An. Idiot.

"This will blow over," Mum continues through the door. "I promise. Stuff like this happens to me all the time. It's always fine in the end."

"Oh really?" I huff. "Stuff just like this happens to you?"

There's a pause. "Well, not *exactly*. But similar! Please open the door so we can talk about it. Come on, you have to eat something. Dinner is on the table!"

I don't reply. I am not opening the door. I do not want to talk about it right now. It's too soon. Every time I think about it, my face grows hot and I have to scream into my pillow.

Here's what happened.

This morning, I was invited to look round a newly refurbished library in London and afterwards say a few words about the importance of libraries in a local school auditorium, to an audience made up of the schools in the area, so about five hundred students. I was very happy to be a part of such a wonderful event.

In front of Jackson and Izzy this morning, Mum suggested that Izzy join me since it's a Saturday and she didn't have any plans. I expected Izzy to say something rude in reply, along the lines of, "I'd rather stick forks in my eyes" – a comment she made the other day when I kindly asked her if she'd like to learn how to play chess. But she actually looked excited and said she'd love to come.

"As long as you don't mind, Pearl," she said, all innocently.

And I fell for it. There I was thinking she'd stand quietly behind me all day, seeing a little of what I do. Instead, I walked right into her horrible prank that she'd clearly been waiting to play on me all week.

I heard some strange gasps from the headmistress and teachers sitting behind me as I stood up to go to the lectern to address my five-hundred-strong audience, but I didn't think anything of it. Then I noticed some giggles from the students when, a couple of minutes into my speech, I turned my back to them in order to gesture to the librarian who was sitting with Izzy and the teachers behind me. She attempted to signal something to me, but I thought she was being overly enthusiastic about me acknowledging her in the speech.

The giggles from the audience became louder. I turned back to the teachers and librarian to see if they could shed some light on the matter. Flashes went off from camera phones in the audience. The giggles turned into raucous laughter and suddenly an entire auditorium of people was laughing at me.

It was at that point that Beth, who had been busy working on her iPad, looked up and saw the problem, rushing over to me and hastily pointing out what was going on.

There was a piece of paper taped to my back with "LOSER" written across it in bold black marker pen. Izzy sat there with a big smirk on her face the whole time. She had patted my back right before I went on stage, wishing me luck.

"Pearl." Mum knocks on the door louder this time. "I know you're upset, but what have I told you about hiding from your problems? You have to face them head on."

I pull the duvet away from my face and stare up at the ceiling. Rosy takes the opportunity to give me a big lick across the forehead.

"Jackson has promised he'll talk to her, OK?" Mum continues.

"It doesn't matter if he talks to her! It is all over the

internet! Pictures and even a video! The whole world is laughing at me!"

"That's not true! It was a silly, thoughtless prank. I promise it won't happen again. Please, Pearl, open the door."

Oh yes, *that* won't happen again because I won't let it, but SOMETHING will. Izzy has been playing pranks on me all week, the "LOSER" sign is simply the latest in a string of targeted attacks of which I have been the innocent victim.

I told Mum straight away this arrangement wasn't going to work. I told her we did not get on. I told her that Jackson and Izzy should not move in. Ever. But Mum insisted it was all going to be fine, she promised that everything would work out in the end and that if I could give Izzy the benefit of the doubt, I would see that she's as great a person as I am.

What a load of RUBBISH.

Izzy is ruining everything! She moved into the house and immediately started complaining about anything she could think of. The food, her mattress, the interior design. At dinner on their first night she said we should take down all the pictures from the staircase because she "didn't like being stared at by random dead people".

Random?! The pictures on the staircase are all the

past Prime Ministers! And the recent ones aren't even dead!

I don't know why Mum insists on being so patient with her when she's so rude to Mum any chance she gets. When Mum tries to make conversation with her, Izzy rarely gives anything more than one-word answers. She acts so coldly towards her, as though all of this is Mum's fault. At least I'm nice to Jackson, no matter how upset about the situation I am. It's called *manners*. Apparently Izzy doesn't have any.

She wears her headphones all the time, so she purposefully can't hear anything anyone says to her. Tony caught her sliding down the bannister and asked her not to, and she completely ignored him! She blares loud music from her room that seems to make the whole house shake and when Mum asked her not to do that because she had very important meetings going on downstairs, she waited until the meetings ended and then turned her speakers right back up again!

And do you know what else? We have to take LESSONS together. Apparently, Izzy wasn't doing so great at her school, so according to Jackson and Mum, it made complete sense for Izzy to give home-schooling a try and join me in my lessons. It's a total FIASCO.

She disrupts every single lesson, she never lets

me speak or ask questions, and she finds it so hard to concentrate that she always goes off point. I don't know how the tutors are coping with this change but it's greatly affecting my work. When I pointed this out to Mum, she got all high and mighty on me and reminded me that I was incredibly lucky to have had one-to-one tutoring up until this point.

"It's nice to have a classmate, isn't it?" she said, before being rushed off by Gabrielle to whatever telephone call she was late for.

It is NOT nice having a classmate, not this one anyway. She pinged an elastic band at my head yesterday when I was in the middle of giving a presentation on the Industrial Revolution. It threw me off and I messed up the last few slides.

"If you want to be Prime Minister one day, Pearl," she said haughtily after I yelled at her for ruining my speech, "then you have to get used to thinking on your feet and carrying on despite distractions. If you think about it, by pinging elastic bands at you mid-talk, I'm *helping* you become the best public speaker you can be. That's a life lesson right there."

Seriously. WHO IS THIS PERSON?

She was rude about my P.E. lesson, too, asking why I didn't play any sports. I told her that I did plenty of physical activity thank you very much, including running and yoga, with an instructor who comes in four times a week and is on hand for all Downing Street staff. Mum thinks it's very important to make sure her colleagues have the opportunity to exercise should they need a break, as it's good for both physical and mental health.

"Yeah, but you're not Downing Street staff," Izzy said when I explained this. "Why don't you join a local sports club where you can do team stuff? Rather than spend all your time doing yoga with old people."

"The Downing Street staff aren't old!"

"You know what I mean."

"I like my current exercise routine," I told her sternly. "Feel free to do your own thing if you wish. Otherwise you're welcome to join the lessons with my instructor."

You see how nice I am to her? I invited her to join in! And did she? Of course not.

Instead of being nice back, like a normal human being, she keeps playing horrible pranks on me. In fact, the only time she really bothers to speak to me tends to be when I fall into another of her traps and she howls with laughter and goes, "You should have seen your face!"

She found out that I'm not a fan of snakes – I don't know who told her about this yet, but when I find out, they are in BIG trouble – and she bought a fake rubber one and keeps leaving it for me to find. In the middle of hallways, in the bath, in the garden.

Yesterday she left it in my BED!

I'm certain I had a minor heart attack, no matter what the Downing Street doctor says.

At lunch the other day, she just yelled, "SNAKE!" in the middle of a civilized conversation, and I screamed at the top of my lungs, jumping up and knocking my bowl, spilling soup all down my front. Apparently, that was HILARIOUS.

Well, the "LOSER" sign is the last straw.

"THIS IS THE LAST STRAW!" I yell to Mum, still refusing to open the door. "She's crossed a line!"

"Pearl, please come have some dinner. She wants to apologize."

"HA!"

"I'm being serious. She really does want to apologize. And I have to get back to work in about half an hour, so please come out so we can eat together. I don't want to leave you upset like this."

Rosy lets out a long, weary sigh.

"I agree," I say gently to her, stroking her head.

"Pearl," Mum pleads.

Reluctantly, I climb out of bed, still in my clothes from earlier in the day, and I stomp across my bedroom to open the door. Rosy hops off the bed, stretches and scampers out. Mum's leaning against the door frame. She gives me a sympathetic look.

"I'll come out my room, but not for her," I say pointedly. "For you."

"Thanks," Mum says, enveloping me in a hug. "You're the strongest person I know."

"Yeah, well, I got it from my mum."

As I pull away from her, I start when I notice someone on the stairs. Izzy is watching us with a funny look on her face. When she realizes I've seen her, she seems embarrassed and clears her throat, coming up the last few steps.

"Hi, Pearl," she begins.

I cross my arms, staring her down.

"Look, I'm really sorry about today," she says, shifting uncomfortably. "I hope you can forgive me."

I raise my eyebrows at her. "That's it?"

A flash of irritation crosses her face, but she must remember the severity of her actions because it's gone as quickly as it came and she's back to doing puppy-dog eyes.

"No, of course I have more to say. I didn't realize that people would take pictures and the incident would end up online. I was told there were no photographers and I thought it would be a bit of fun. Lighten the atmosphere. I thought—"

"You thought humiliating me on a national scale would be a bit of fun?"

"All right, Pearl," Mum says gently, "let her finish her apology."

"Thank you, Patrice," Izzy says, blinking up at her gratefully, all doe-eyed.

Oh, PLEASE. That's the nicest thing she's said to Mum in forever. She's playing her! Well, she won't be able to manipulate me so easily. There's nothing she could say that would make me even CONSIDER forgiving her.

"What I did was immature and wrong," she continues. "I sincerely apologize and will never do anything like that again. If it makes you feel any better, Beth told me that your popularity has gone up."

"She . . . she said that?"

"Yeah." Izzy nods vigorously. "Because you handled it so gracefully, laughing at the sign when you realized and then walking off the stage smiling. Apparently, your reaction has gone down very well with the public."

"Really? Huh."

I mean, I do think I handled the situation quite well.

Like that actor Mum and I saw in an open-air production of Shakespeare's *Hamlet*. A bird pooped on his shoulder in the middle of the scene and, when the audience gasped, he looked at it in disdain and said, "How I loathe winged creatures," before carrying on perfectly with his lines.

He wasn't a big part, but he got a standing ovation at the curtain call.

"Thank you for your apology, Isabella," I say eventually, lifting my chin.

She winces at me using her full name but doesn't correct me. Whoops. I know she doesn't like being called Isabella but I keep forgetting. I'm not about to say sorry to her, anyway, not after today. She'll just have to let that one go.

"You're lucky I have such a great sense of humour," I add.

She nods slowly. "Right. That's true."

"Great." Mum smiles in relief, squeezing my shoulders. "I know this is a lot of change, but I'm so proud of both of you for how brilliantly you're handling it."

Izzy purses her lips. I drop my eyes to the floor, biting my tongue. Mum checks her watch and encourages us to head down to dinner so she can grab something to eat with us before her next meeting.

I go to bed that night feeling a little better than I did this afternoon. What Izzy did was unacceptable, but she *did* apologize. As Mum says, apologies are never easy. So I do appreciate it.

Hopefully, things will be a bit brighter tomorrow.

"Oh!" Tony clasps a hand over his mouth as I emerge from my bedroom in the morning, on my way to the bathroom.

I yawn. "I know I never look my best when I've just woken up, Tony, but it's a little rude to point it out so obviously."

He shakes his head, saying in a strained voice, "Y-your eyebrows."

"What? What about them?"

Startled by his horrified expression, I run to the bathroom and fling open the door, sliding across the tiles to get to the mirror. I see my reflection.

"AHHHHHHHHHHHHHHHHHHH!!!!" I scream at the top of my voice.

MY EYEBROWS ARE BRIGHT GREEN!!

As I hyperventilate in front of the mirror, Izzy strolls past the bathroom.

"Wow, that's a bold look," she comments, looking unsurprised and smiling to herself. "Lucky you have that great sense of humour."

OK, I feel bad about the eyebrows.

It seemed like a good idea at the time and, don't get me wrong, it was genuinely HILARIOUS to see Perfect Pearl with lime-green eyebrows, and it's not like it couldn't be fixed, she obviously had a beautician on speed dial who came and sorted it out. But it's hard not to feel bad when I saw how upset she was.

Pranking her isn't the nicest thing to do, but she really needs to learn to laugh at herself. I feel like I'm doing her a favour in the long run. It's like she's a robot or something, she can't relax and have fun. Everything has to be scheduled in and noted down. She can't go with the flow or leave things up to chance. If anything is just a little bit off, she flies off the handle.

I feel sorry for her assistant.

Which, by the way, is nuts in itself. What kind of thirteen-year-old needs an assistant? Maybe if you're Naomi Starr and you're a famous popstar, but Pearl? Is she really so in-demand that she needs Beth to keep a schedule for her? It's like she goes out of her way to be busy, as though she can't bear to chill out on her own.

And the whole time I've been here, she hasn't hung out with friends once.

I am SO EXCITED to escape this place tonight and meet up with Jenna and Kylie to go to a concert. I haven't been able to do anything I want for AGES. All the stuff I've been invited to recently by my old school friends, like cinema and shopping trips, I've had to turn down because of everything going on with Dad and Patrice. It's all been a bit mad.

But tonight I get to see my friends and be myself again. Finally, some NORMALITY. I am so fed up with having to walk around on eggshells, abide by all these stupid rules. I hate living here.

In Downing Street, you can't get away with doing your own thing. I get in trouble at least once a day for doing something bad, being somewhere I shouldn't or saying the wrong thing. You have to be so careful and quiet all the time in case you disturb an important meeting.

I got told off for playing my music too loud, so I started using my headphones and then I got told off for ignoring people because I couldn't hear them. I get funny looks from the ministers and I know it's to do with my clothes, like no one here is allowed to have a sense of style. I am NOT going to start dressing like

Pearl. You know what she was wearing yesterday? A trouser suit. With a blazer and everything. A TROUSER SUIT. I was in a T-shirt and shorts.

"Interesting outfit choice," I said with, admittedly, a hint of sarcasm when I saw her.

"It's called power dressing," she snarled back. "You should dress for the job you want, Izzy, not the job you have."

"I don't have a job, Pearl, I'm thirteen. And in case you forgot, you are too."

Then she rolled her eyes and marched away from me.

Ugh. Pearl is the worst.

Anyway, I basically can't get anything right living here. I don't fit in at all, and the only person making me feel welcome isn't a person at all, she's a dog. Rosy loves me, partly because I give her lots of attention and partly because I slip her food under the table.

I also can't step out the front door without having my picture taken. It is SO annoying. I feel like I'm always being watched, nothing is private. Dad's trying to make out as though not much has changed. He's doing his best to keep things normal and make it a bit homelier, but he's failing miserably.

"Family movie night?" he said brightly one morning. "What do you say?"

"Great!" I replied cheerfully. We've always done movie night at least once a week. It's one of my favourite things to do with Dad and I've missed it.

"What film is it?" Pearl asked, not bothering to look up from her book.

I waited for Dad to say something like, "Oh sorry, Pearl, family movie night is mine and Izzy's thing," but instead he said to her, "Why don't you pick?" as though he was HAPPY about her joining.

I didn't say anything at the time, but as soon as Dad and I were on our own later, I let him have it, demanding that he tell her she couldn't join.

"But it's family movie night," he said, his brow furrowed as though I was the one being weird. "That means everyone together."

"They are NOT my family," I huffed.

"No, I know," he said, glancing down at his shoes. "But it's important that we all do things together. Good bonding time."

"I don't want to bond with Pearl."

"Why don't you try giving her a chance?" he said calmly. "I know you're both different, but you also have lots in common."

"We have nothing in common. She's a snotty-nosed brat. We'll never see eye to eye."

"Maybe put yourself in her shoes," he said, lowering his voice so no one around could hear. "Imagine if your parent was the Prime Minister."

"Imagine if my parent was DATING the Prime Minister," I replied, crossing my arms stubbornly. "Oh no, wait, I don't have to imagine. I'm living that nightmare."

Dad looked a bit dejected at that comment, but I stayed strong. He needed to know that it wasn't easy for me living here.

"All I'm saying is that there's a lot of pressure on her shoulders, and this isn't just a sudden thing," he explained wearily. "She's been in the public eye for a while, during the whole campaign. It's not like she had her dad to lean on. She had to stand by her mum's side and be strong for her, all on her own." He hesitated, looking me in the eye. "You know how hard that can be. You certainly have that in common."

I looked away from him.

"Fine," I sighed. "We can do movie night together."

"Thanks, Izzy," he said, ruffling my hair. "I really

appreciate everything you're doing to make this work."

But it was no use. Movie night was rubbish.

The popcorn was posh and tasted funny, Pearl asked irritating questions the whole way through the film, going on about plot holes and what wasn't realistic, while Patrice pretended to be watching but was on her emails the whole time and kept having to go out and take calls.

I hate that everything has changed. I hate it. I hate all of it.

I don't belong at 10 Downing Street. I never will.

CHAPTER EIGHT

"Where do you think you're going?"

Izzy stops in her tracks as she passes my bedroom door and turns to face me with a sullen expression. Admittedly, my question may have come out a little snarkier than I meant it to. I'm actually just genuinely intrigued as to where she's off to because she's dressed up to go out, but it came out a bit patronizing. I blame this on Izzy. She forces me into a bossy, grown-up role because she's so childish and immature.

"I'm going to a concert," she says proudly, sticking her chin out, "with my *friends*."

"What kind of concert?" I ask indifferently, turning the page of my book before going back to petting Rosy, who is curled up on my duvet next to me.

I don't know why I'm bothering to ask her any questions about her stupid social life. It's not like I care what she's doing. As far as I'm concerned it will be nice to get her out of the house. And she's acting as though I should be jealous, but why would I want to go to any kind of concert that Izzy's interested in? She has terrible taste.

I haven't forgiven her in the slightest for the eyebrow incident. I begged Mum for a lock on my door, but she refused, which, in my opinion, is ridiculous.

I asked her how she'd like it if I dyed her eyebrows in the middle of the night.

She pointed out that she has agents on her door while she sleeps, so there's no chance I'd get in. I asked if I could have an agent on MY door, since I was the one who was attacked.

She said no to that too. Honestly, Mum is SO unfair.

"We're going to see an amazing band called Coasting," Izzy replies. "They're up-and-coming, you won't have heard of them."

"Is 'up-and-coming' code for no one's heard of them because they're really bad?"

She narrows her eyes at me. "It means they're different and unusual and cool. And my friends and I managed to get tickets before they hit the big time. Their single is climbing up the charts as we speak. We're true fans, we liked them before they were famous."

"Congratulations."

"Let me guess, you'll be spending the night reading."

"I have homework to do. We have that French test tomorrow. By the way, did you tell my mum about this concert?"

"Why should I?" she says defensively. "I told Dad about it ages ago, so he knows. I don't have to tell *your* mum anything to do with me."

"You should probably remind him then, so he can tell Mum the details," I advise, closing my book and looking at her with a serious expression. "Mum will need to know what the venue is and who you're going with. You really need to tell her stuff like this way in advance."

"It's strange," Izzy sighs, bored, "you look like a teenager but you talk like an old person. I'll see you later."

As she leaves, waltzing away down the corridor, I swing my legs off the bed and follow her, Rosy bounding along at my feet.

"I mean it, Izzy," I say. "You can't just head out whenever you feel like it."

"Yes, I can," she calls back, sounding irritated as she traipses down the stairs. "It's called having a life. You should try it some time."

"That's not how it works. There are protocols, you have to run things by—"

"Blah, blah, blah," she interrupts loudly, jumping down the last couple of steps. "I'm not listening to you any more."

Luckily, Mum comes out of a meeting right at that moment and almost marches straight into Izzy as she crosses the hall. Both Gabrielle and Sebastian are with her and as Mum stops suddenly, they bump into each other like dominoes.

Sebastian looks furious at such an inconvenience.

"Whoops!" Mum laughs, both her and Izzy stopping just in time before a collision. "Sorry, that was rather a tense meeting and I came storming out here on a mission. You look nice, Izzy."

"Thank you," Izzy says sharply, before continuing towards the door.

"Where are you going?" Mum asks loudly. "It's late."

Izzy reluctantly turns around. "It's not a big deal, I'm going to a concert with some friends. I told Dad about it ages ago."

"Hang on." Mum walks towards her. "What concert? Who's going with you? I didn't know about this. Gabrielle –" she glances over her shoulder at her PA – "can you find Jackson please?"

Gabrielle nods and hurries off.

"It is NOT a big deal," Izzy says again through gritted

teeth. "It's just a small concert with my friends. We're going in a group and I won't be back late. Not that it's any of your business, because you're not my parent. OK? Great. Bye then."

"Izzy," Mum begins carefully as Izzy approaches the front door, "I need to make sure everything is in place before you go."

"Like what? This isn't official business. I'm going out with my friends. Does no one else in this building know the concept of *having friends?*" Her eyes flash angrily at me as I watch from the stairs. I feel my cheeks flush with embarrassment. "We don't need to have an official meeting about it."

"What's going on?" Jackson says, appearing with Gabrielle. "Izzy, where are you going? Why are you all dressed up?"

"What is WRONG with everyone?" Izzy cries, exasperated. "Dad, I told you I was going to the Coasting concert and you said I could go."

"I remember you getting tickets." Jackson frowns. "But that was a while ago. You didn't tell me what date it was."

"OK, well, it's today." Izzy checks her phone. "I have to go, my friends are waiting nearby and we're going to be late."

"Tell your friends to come here," Mum instructs, gesturing for Maya to come over from where she is standing just a few feet away. "And you need to tell Maya about the concert, where the venue is and so on. She'll need details to prep her security team."

"Security team? What?" Izzy looks appalled. "What are you talking about?"

"Izzy, you can't just go to a concert without telling anyone," Jackson says, running a hand through his hair. "We need to make sure it's secure and that you'll be safe. You're in the public eye now, sweetheart. We need all the facts before you go and you'll need to have some members of security with you. It's protocol."

"This is so stupid. I'm going and you can't stop me."

"*Izzy*," Jackson says authoritatively, before she can storm away. "You cannot go *yet*. Tell your friends to come here."

"Dad!"

"Tell them to come here," he repeats in an impressively stern voice. "I'm not stopping you from going to the concert. We need to make sure it's safe first, that's all."

"I can't tell them to come here," she says, pleadingly. "It's so embarrassing! I refuse."

"We'll wait with you until they get here," Mum says in that voice she uses when there's absolutely no chance of arguing with her and you both know it, before addressing Maya. "The band playing tonight is called Coasting."

Izzy looks as though she might explode with the unfairness of it all, but instead settles on letting out a loud "ARGH" in irritation before angrily calling her friend Kylie and explaining the situation.

"I know, it is so ANNOYING," she seethes down the phone, loud enough for everyone to hear. "I am so sorry about this, but I swear we won't miss the band. It will be, like, one minute. I'm so sorry. This is so EMBARRASSING. I've tried to get out of it. I know, I know. I'm sorry. I really am, Kylie. Thanks, I'll see you in a bit."

She hangs up and then crosses her arms, while Maya goes off to make some calls. Jackson and Mum share a look as Izzy taps her foot impatiently.

Sebastian clears his throat, obviously unable to put up with this any longer. "Prime Minister, we really have a lot to get on with—"

"Please do go ahead and start the transport meeting without me, Sebastian," Mum instructs. "I will join you once things here have been sorted."

"But—"

"Thank you, Sebastian," she says, cutting him off

and giving him a look that means there will be no more questions.

Inhaling deeply and pursing his lips, Sebastian strides off, disappearing through a door down the hall. Rosy growls at his back as he goes.

"It's as though you're trying to ruin everything good about my life on purpose," Izzy snaps, glaring at Jackson. "I've had to change everything, leave my home, leave my school, *everything*. It's one concert with my friends, one NORMAL evening to do what I want to do for once, and you can't even let me have that."

"I'm sorry you feel that way, Izzy," Mum begins. "We're not trying to take away—"

"I wasn't talking to you," Izzy interrupts.

"Izzy," Jackson warns, "don't speak to Patrice like that."

"It's OK," Mum says hurriedly.

"I have two agents available," Maya says, coming over to update Mum. "They're gathering all the information about the concert and getting in touch with the venue managers now. They'll bring a car around once Izzy's friends have arrived and after the concert can drop them off at their respective homes after Izzy has returned here."

"Great, thank you, Maya."

"Wait, what?" Izzy's jaw drops to the floor. "Are you serious? *Two agents?* They're not coming to the concert."

"Yes, they are," Jackson replies.

"Dad, NO."

"They'll blend in," Mum insists gently. "They're professionals."

"Is this some kind of joke?" Izzy looks from Mum to Jackson, completely baffled. "I'm not the Prime Minister! Nobody cares about me! Why are you doing this? What exactly do you expect to happen?"

"As your dad said, you're now in the public eye and that means we have to take certain precautions," Mum explains calmly. "You might easily be recognized and it's our job to make sure that you feel safe and never find yourself in an uncomfortable situation."

"So you're taking away my freedom?" Izzy retorts spitefully. "You're sending babysitters to watch me?"

"You won't notice them," I offer, leaning against the bannister. "They don't stand that close to you and you sort of forget they're there at all."

From Izzy's thunderous expression, I wish I hadn't said anything at all. But thankfully, just as she opens her mouth to likely say something rude to me, there's a knock at the door and the custodian opens it to allow in two girls. Izzy rushes over to greet them and immediately begins apologizing. I don't get it. Why is she saying sorry? Most people would LOVE to have the opportunity to come here. But Izzy is acting as though she's somehow ruined their night.

Rosy doesn't help matters either, running over to welcome them, but neither seems interested. I hear one of them mutter, "She won't slobber on my shoes, right?" as she bats Rosy away.

While Izzy is busy saying sorry over and over to her friends, Mum whispers something to Jackson and then sneaks away. I guess Izzy's friends might feel a bit overwhelmed meeting the Prime Minister without any warning. They already look thrown, standing in the middle of the reception hall at 10 Downing Street, having set off this evening simply to go to a concert.

Putting myself in their shoes and acknowledging how awkward and surreal this must be, I decide to make them feel welcome. I skip down the stairs and head over to them with a warm smile.

"Hello, and welcome to 10 Downing Street," I say, holding out my hand for them to shake.

Izzy recoils the moment I approach, while her two friends seem startled, shaking my hand limply. I step back, wondering why Izzy is shooting daggers at me.

"Dad, we're going to go now," she says hurriedly, ushering them back to the door even though they've only just come in. "The car is here, yeah?"

"As if you live here," Kylie says, looking around. "It's all very . . . old."

I know it's Kylie because Izzy has been mainly aiming her apologies at her. Kylie seems to be the queen bee of this group and is acting unimpressed by the whole situation.

"The house is old, but it has a really cool history," I pitch in enthusiastically. "Prime Ministers have worked here since 1735 and—"

"We really have to go," Izzy interrupts, sounding disgusted, while the other two girls share a look. "Let's head to the car."

"Did you say 'a really *cool* history'?" Jenna says, stifling a laugh.

Kylie giggles next to her and Izzy closes her eyes in despair.

My cheeks grow hot. "I meant—"

"Bye, everyone!" Izzy practically yells, looking mortified.

"Maya and I will come out with you," Jackson says, giving the door custodian a nod. "We can go through details about the agents in the car."

"Agents?" Kylie says, raising her eyebrows. "Like security agents? What's going on, Izzy?"

"I'll explain, it's not a big deal, it will be fine," she says, flustered, ushering them out as the door is opened for them and camera flashes immediately start going off across the road. "Everything will be normal. I promise."

IZZY'S BLOG

It's official. That was the worst night of my life.

I'm never talking to my dad again. All he had to do was let me have one night of normality. ONE NIGHT. But no, that wasn't allowed. Nothing is allowed any more. No fun, no friends, no life. None of it is allowed when your dad is dating the Prime Minister.

And what is with Pearl?! It's like she can't do anything without making a situation TEN TIMES WORSE.

She HAD to come over and offer Jenna and Kylie a HANDSHAKE when they came in, just to make sure they were as uncomfortable as possible. As though they weren't already freaking out about how formal and weird the situation is, she comes over like the queen of the world, welcoming her lowly subjects to her big, intimidating house. Why can't she just say "hey" like a normal person?! Why did she have to greet them at all?!

I have never been more embarrassed. Jenna kept doing impressions of her in the car afterwards and Kylie was shrieking with laughter.

I had to laugh along too, but it was so weird because Hal was driving us and I know he always drives Pearl, and, even though he didn't say anything, he kept catching my eye in the rearview mirror as though I was being a bad person.

EXCUSE ME, HAL, BUT I AM THE ONLY NORMAL PERSON IN THIS SCENARIO.

Things only got worse after that.

I managed to persuade Maya to let just ONE agent escort us to the concert because, come on, it's not like I'm Patrice or Pearl or Dad, no one really knows who I am. Sure, they might vaguely recognize me, but the press hasn't exactly splashed my face all over the place. I haven't done anything interesting enough for that because I'm not allowed to do anything interesting at all.

The "LOSER" sign did catch their attention, but they were more focused on Pearl's reaction than me. To be honest, I'm not sure I've come out of that looking so good.

Anyway, Maya had to admit that I wasn't exactly a big fish, so one agent was more than enough. She assigned me one of her "top agents" who followed in the car behind and didn't say a word as he came over to join us when we climbed out the car. He was wearing jeans and a T-shirt with a black leather jacket and he didn't take off his sunglasses the whole time.

Yeah, sure, Pearl, he blended right in. HELLO, he couldn't have looked MORE like a secret service agent! It was like he'd walked out from auditioning for a movie role of "Prime Minister's undercover security agent". Not to mention, everyone else at the concert was a teenager.

"I hope people don't think we've brought our dad along," Kylie said, looking at Jenna who nodded loyally. "It's SO embarrassing."

"Pretend he's not there," I said quickly. "Do you want a drink? Coke with extra ice, right? I'll get three!"

I queued up at the drinks stand, glancing back at Jenna and Kylie, who were huddled together, talking in low voices and sniggering. I tried to ignore it and focus on having a good time, free from the confines of Downing Street. But it was hard not to feel like they were making fun of me. It's so unfair, none of this is MY FAULT.

It took me a long time to get in with Jenna and Kylie. They've always been the most popular girls in the school and I had to work hard to be accepted into their exclusive group. Say all the right things, be good at all the right stuff. And I like hanging out with them. We always have so much fun when we're together.

But who wants to be friends with someone who has a long list of rules, can't step a toe out of line and comes with a bodyguard? Look at Pearl. No one is friends with her because of all these reasons.

That, and the fact she's so WEIRD.

I got the drinks and we decided to head into the venue because the band was about to come on. Our tickets were standing ones, which we got specifically so we could go right to the front of the stage, but just as we were about to get stuck into the crowd the agent was like, "I'd prefer it if you could stick nearer to an exit."

Jenna and Kylie looked shocked, so I jumped in quickly and said, "No way, we're going to the front," and just started barging through the crowd without looking back. They followed me to a good spot, right in the middle, the agent lurking behind us, his forehead creased in irritation. Whatever. I didn't care. This was my life and I wasn't going to let him ruin it.

"Maybe you should go stand at the back," Kylie said to me after a few moments of awkward silence between the three of us. "It's kind of weird, him standing right there."

"Yeah, I feel like I can't relax," Jenna agreed.

"I don't want people thinking he's with us," Kylie added. "We can meet you after maybe."

I looked at them, hurt, because yes it was annoying, but I'd told them a hundred times in the car that I didn't want any of this, but it's not exactly easy to fight with Dad, let alone the Prime Minister.

But I didn't have a chance to say anything, because next thing you know there's a loud bang from the stage.

Usually, people would go, "What was that?" and then carry on with their normal, fun lives when they realized it was nothing.

But that's not what happens when you have a bodyguard.

The agent heard the bang and leapt into action. He threw his arm around me and in the process knocked Jenna and Kylie's large Cokes all over them.

They screamed as the icy liquid splashed down their clothes.

But I couldn't apologize, as I was being dragged out of the concert, the agent yelling, "OUT THE WAY! MOVE!" to the crowd parting to let us through, wondering what was going on.

Hal was waiting in the car right outside the building, so the agent opened the door, shoved me in the car and then said, "Drive" to Hal as he jumped in after me, slammed the door shut and off we sped.

"WHAT DO YOU THINK YOU'RE DOING?" I yelled, but the agent paid no attention to me because he was too busy listening to his earpiece.

Eventually, he went, "Uh-huh. Yep. Good. Roger that," to whoever he was in contact with, then turned to me and said, "The vicinity has been checked and it was a malfunctioning stage pyrotechnic. We can now return to the concert."

"WHAT IS WRONG WITH YOU?" I shouted, furious.

He didn't seem in the least bit fazed. He stared back at me with a neutral expression. I guess much scarier people have yelled in his face before.

I got out my phone and quickly called Kylie as Hal turned the car round. She didn't pick up so I tried

Jenna. She didn't pick up either, so I tried Kylie again. Eventually, she answered.

"Hello?"

She did not sound happy. She sounded FURIOUS.

"Kylie, I'm so sorry. The agent majorly overreacted and—"

"My outfit is RUINED. So is Jenna's! That was so embarrassing! Why did you have to run out like that? Do you think you're some kind of celebrity now? Are we beneath you or something?"

"Kylie, no! You know I don't think like that!"

"We never see you any more, you never come to anything we invite you to, and now, because of you, our night is ruined and you just left us here without even saying sorry!"

"The agent grabbed me, there was nothing I could do. Kylie, you—"

"It was literally a sound effect. So obvious. Like, nothing even happened."

"I know and I'm so, so sorry," I pleaded, feeling like I was going to cry, "but I promise I'll make it up to you. Now that they know it was nothing, I can come back and—"

"I don't think that's a good idea, Izzy. It's just too much drama with you here."

"What? No, it won't be—"

"Just leave it. My top is all wet and— Oh my god, they're coming on! I've got to go."

I heard the crowd in the background go wild as the band came on the stage. Kylie hung up before I could even say goodbye.

CHAPTER NINE

Izzy is ignoring almost everyone in the house.

Personally, I think it's a very welcome development. She's been shut up in her room for the past few days, avoiding us at any cost, which I think should be encouraged. She won't engage with any of our school lessons, which means I can actually hear myself think and can ask the tutors questions without being laughed at. And when her dad finally forced her to sit and eat dinner with us, she wouldn't say one word. Not one.

It's wonderful.

"You should try talking to her," Tony suggested yesterday, while I studied the chessboard.

I moved my bishop. "Who?"

"Izzy," he said, taking one of my pawns with his knight. "She's having a tough time."

"I've tried to make an effort with her and she wants nothing to do with me. I'm not going to waste my time reaching out to someone who hates me."

"She doesn't hate you," he said, taking a sip of tea. "She's new. It's hard being new."

"Tony," I began sternly, moving my queen, "we're all new to this situation. She's been going out of her way to make it worse for herself. Have you already forgotten the green-eyebrows incident?"

He tried his best not to smile, but to no avail. I glared at him.

"Come on, it was a *little* funny," he said, moving his queen. "I get that she shouldn't have done it, but at the same time, isn't it nice to have someone to play pranks with? Someone your own age to hang out with?"

I sighed, moving my rook determinedly before leaning back in my chair. "Why does everyone think we should be friends just because we're the same age? We have nothing in common and she's made it clear she hates it here. If Mum and Jackson were smart, they'd realize that the best thing for everyone is for Jackson and Izzy to move out. Things were much better the way they were. She keeps ruining everything."

"Change can be good," Tony offered, examining the board. "It brings new challenges. We may not want them at first, but more often than not, those challenges nudge us in the right direction."

I rolled my eyes. "Not this time."

"Sometimes, we don't realize what's right in front of us." He moved his queen and grinned at me. "Checkmate."

I was so shocked, I sat up abruptly and spilled my tea all over the board. That will teach me for allowing him to distract me with deep and meaningful conversations when I should be focused on my game.

He's wrong anyway. Izzy doesn't want anyone to talk to her. She wants to be alone. The other day she saw me brushing my teeth in the bathroom, so stomped in, snatched her toothbrush from the pot and went to the hassle of brushing her teeth in her bedroom, only coming back in briefly to spit. She doesn't want to be anywhere near me for even the shortest of moments.

She's angriest at Mum, I think. I know Mum's tried talking to her but Izzy has given her the cold shoulder. She blames her for what happened at the concert, because if Mum weren't Prime Minister then none of the security would be necessary. But really, it's bad luck. If that sound thing hadn't gone wrong on stage and caused a bang, there wouldn't have been an issue. It's not Mum's fault. If anything, it's nice that she cares so much about Izzy's safety.

"She doesn't see it that way, I'm afraid," Mum said when I ranted about Izzy behaving so irrationally. "She resents me."

"She's so ungrateful."

"Hey." Mum frowned at me. "She has a right to be angry. There's been a lot of change for her."

Seriously, why is everyone yabbering on about the big changes for Izzy? What about ME?! Everything was going very smoothly until she barged into my life with her horrible pranks and permanently unimpressed expression.

"I wish she'd talk to me," Mum said then, all quiet and vulnerable. "I want to make it better."

I didn't like the way she said that, to be honest. My mum isn't the moping type and she always has the answers to everything. So seeing her genuinely upset about Izzy shutting her out made me feel . . . sad. And there was nothing I could do to help. That made me feel terrible.

You see? Izzy is ruining everything.

"I have an idea," Jackson announces, while I'm pouring myself some orange juice in the kitchen and musing over Izzy's behaviour the last few days since the concert. "Pearl, how would you feel about Izzy joining you on your visit to the . . . uh . . . where was it you're going this afternoon again?"

"A trampoline park. And I do not feel good about Izzy joining me. So, no. See you."

"Wait, wait," he says, stopping me at the door. "Hear me out. I know you and Izzy don't see eye to eye yet—"

"Ever," I correct.

"—but she could do with some cheering up," he continues, ignoring my comment, "and no one can be sad at a trampoline park, right? You're literally bouncing up! You can't possibly be down!"

"Jackson, I love the metaphor and everything, but honestly I think it will make things worse."

"It's North London, isn't it? It's right by where we used to live. She can show you some of her favourite haunts."

I blink at him. "What, like grotty music venues? Ew. No thanks."

"It would be really good for her to get out her room."

"She comes out for our lessons and that's quite enough, thank you."

"Pearl. *Please.*"

I don't know, maybe it's the way he's looking at me, all sad and tired, but I feel that I should help him. It's not going to work, if anything it will make her angrier, but that can't be blamed on me. I'm acting on instruction.

I sigh heavily. "Fine."

"Thank you, thank you," he says, his eyes lighting up.

We walk out the kitchen and up the stairs together, reaching Izzy's room where Jackson tentatively knocks on the door. As expected, she doesn't answer, so he pushes the door open and pops his head through.

"Hey, mind if we come in?"

There's no answer. He opens it wide enough for me to step into her room with him. She is lying on the bed with her headphones on, scrolling through her phone. There are clothes and shoes strewn across the floor.

I glance around at the mess, trying desperately not to say anything negative because I don't want to fuel the flames, but someone REALLY needs to tell her about the Tidy Room, Tidy Mind theory. No wonder she finds it hard to concentrate.

"Izzy, can you take your headphones off for a second?"

Jackson motions for her to remove them, but she pretends not to see. Eventually he picks his way across her room and pulls them off her ears. She scowls up at him.

"What?" she snaps.

"You need to get out this room," he says firmly. "Pearl

is going to visit a trampoline park this afternoon and we thought you could join her."

"No thanks," she says, reaching for her headphones, but he pulls them away from her grasp.

"Come on, it will be fun. Right, Pearl?"

"Yes," I say, trying not to be distracted by the large pile of crumpled clothes on her desk chair that looks as though it might topple over any second. "It's all to do with Mum's brilliant campaign for promoting fun, healthy exercise for children and teenagers."

"Sounds like a blast. I'll pass," she says, deadpan, going back to staring at her phone.

"Izzy," Jackson begins, "you have to stop being mad at—"

"It was the most embarrassing night of my life. I looked like an idiot and I ruined everything for my friends. I wouldn't want to hang out with me if I was them. And, to make things worse, I don't go to school any more, so it's not like I have the chance to spend time with them and explain in person. Sorry, Dad, but I'm going to be mad as long as I like."

"It's Kylie's birthday next week, right?" Jackson says, refusing to give up quite yet. "Is she having a party?"

"I guess she will." Izzy shrugs. "She said she was planning something."

"If you go to the trampoline park with Pearl, I give you my word that you can go to that party, whenever it is, without security."

She looks up at him. "Really? You promise?"

"I promise. It will be completely normal. We won't interfere one bit. You can just go and have fun with your friends. Promise," he repeats, putting his hand on his heart. "The trampoline park is near our flat, so you can go get one of those drinks from that smoothie bar we love so much. Bet you've missed those, right? The strawberry and banana one? The one which you'll only be drinking half of so that I can steal the other half when you get home later? You know the one?"

He nudges her with his elbow. She tries not to smile, but he's got her and they both know it. He nudges her again and she can't help but grin.

"I guess I have missed those smoothies," she admits reluctantly.

"Pearl, can you ask Hal to stop at Greta's Smoothie Bar?" Jackson says, straightening up and beaming at me. "Izzy can show him the way when you're nearby."

"Course," I say, checking my watch. "We should go now, Izzy, so you probably want to change."

She pushes herself up off the bed and looks down at her outfit of tracksuit bottoms and a black jumper that's so old and faded it's gone bobbly and has holes in the sleeves.

"Nah," she says, strolling past me out the room. "I'm good like this."

"Have you been to a trampoline park before?" I ask Izzy after about thirty minutes of excruciating silence on the car journey.

"No," she replies, staring out the window.

"Do you like trampolining?"

"Yes."

It's like pulling teeth. She is ridiculously stubborn. And none of what happened at the concert is even my fault! She is acting like a child and if I wasn't intent on keeping Mum happy by at least being civil, I would tell her so.

"This is a nice area," I say, changing tack and gesturing at the residential road. "Is this near where you lived?"

"Yes."

"What's your house like?"

"Fine."

I give up. It takes all my willpower not to roll my eyes.

"Wow, I can picture it so vividly," I mutter.

We fall back into silence. Hal clears his throat,

obviously uncomfortable with the tension. The agent in the front seat continues to stare straight ahead. At least, I think he does. He's wearing sunglasses so it's hard to tell.

Suddenly, Izzy sits bolt upright and screams, "STOP THE CAR!"

Hal brakes and the security agent swivels in his seat.

"What's wrong?" he demands.

"What the—?" Izzy says, peering out the window, ignoring him.

"Izzy!" I say, irritated. "What is going on? You can't just yell stop—"

"Wait here," she instructs, before undoing her seatbelt, opening the car door and jumping out. She turns to point a finger at the agent who is getting out too and says very pointedly, "Do NOT come with me, everything is fine. I just need to check something."

Hal and the agent look to me for an explanation, but I'm as flabbergasted as they are. I slide quickly along the backseat and get out on her side. She's walking determinedly up the drive to a house which has a mass of colourful balloons tied to its gates.

"You park up. I'll go with her," I assure the agent, before hurrying to catch up as she reaches the door and presses the bell. "Izzy, what are you doing?"

She ignores me, waiting for someone to answer. I can hear music and laughter coming from the garden, so it's unlikely anyone can hear the bell ringing. Izzy must come to the same conclusion. She comes back down the front steps and goes round to the side of the house where there's a gate with another couple of balloons tied to the handle. She pushes it open and starts walking towards the back garden.

"*Izzy!*" I hiss, aware that trespassing is not a good look for the Prime Minister's daughter.

But she marches on. I glance back to see our security agent now standing at the bottom of the drive looking twitchy and I realize that it's better I go after her than he does. I shoot him a big grin and a thumbs up as though everything is completely under control and then I scurry along the path after Izzy.

When I emerge into the garden, I see her standing in front of what looks like a very fun party. There's a DJ and everything, and lots of people our age dancing around the garden or playing games. I gasp in excitement at the giant chessboard, which sadly is being overlooked due to the giant Jenga set right next to it.

I turn my attention back to Izzy and notice that she's staring at someone in the middle of the garden, who is chatting and laughing with a group of girls. She's wearing a birthday tiara and an unnecessarily large badge that says "Birthday Girl".

"Wait," I say, peering at her as she notices us and stops mid-conversation. "Is that *Kylie?*"

Izzy doesn't answer, but it is her. Standing next to Kylie is Jenna. And I'm guessing the other people here, now turning to stare at us, are all of Izzy's school friends.

Uh-oh. This is not going to go well.

"Izzy, what are you doing here?" Kylie demands, striding over with her group of friends in tow. She points at me in a very rude manner. "And why is *she* here?"

"Happy birthday, Kylie," I say with a sincere smile, attempting to keep the peace. "Nice to see you again. Cool badge. And what a lovely garden. Out of interest, where did you get that giant chess set? I'll have to get myself one of those!"

She looks at me as though I'm an alien.

"Your birthday is next week," Izzy says to Kylie, finding her voice. "I thought ... I thought your party would be next weekend."

"Then it would clash with Emily's." Kylie nods to one of the other girls standing near her.

"But. . ." Izzy trails off, looking completely floored.

"Look, Izzy, I couldn't invite you after what happened at the concert," Kylie explains with a sigh, as though annoyed she has to bother justifying it at all. "Emily felt the same way about hers after we told her about it."

"I apologized about that. It wasn't my fault."

"Seriously?" Jenna suddenly gasps, craning to look behind us. "You brought your bodyguard here today, too?"

We turn to see the security agent a couple of metres away, having waited as long as possible to give us the benefit of the doubt. Izzy's face falls.

"No! No, I told him not to come! I swear! I don't want any of this!"

"This is *exactly* why I didn't invite you," Kylie huffs, her entourage nodding sympathetically. "You show up at MY party with your bodyguard and turn it into a big drama all about YOU."

"No, that's not what—"

"You've changed," Jenna says accusingly. "We've invited you to so many things and you didn't come to any of them. It's like you didn't want to make an effort with us any more. You think you're too good for us."

"That's not true!" Izzy says desperately. "I couldn't come to things, just for a bit. With the press and all the attention around. . . I was moving house and it wasn't easy to get out of family things. It's because of my dad and everything that's—"

"Yes, we know, he's dating the Prime Minister," Kylie

says, rolling her eyes. "We thought we were your friends. But it's like you've decided to drop us. It's so boring, Izzy, you rubbing it in that you're some kind of big deal now."

"You are my friends! I don't think I'm a big deal!"

"You can't go to an event without a bodyguard," Jenna points out. "And you live in a big, stuffy house with people who hold open the front door for you."

"That doesn't mean I've changed!"

"Sorry, Izzy, but I think you should go," Kylie huffs. "I don't want you ruining my birthday party, too. Of course, you HAD to come even though you weren't invited and make it all about you."

"Kylie, that's not what's happened," Izzy begins. "Please—"

"Pearl and Izzy, before you go, can I get a selfie?" One of the boys who has been watching the drama unfold steps forward with his phone. "Are you two, like, friends now? After that 'LOSER' sign thing? That was so funny!"

"Oh me too, I would love a picture," squeaks a girl next to him. "I'm a huge fan of your mum, Pearl!"

"Patrice Francis is a major inspiration," another girl says, hurrying forwards to get nearer to us. "She's my idol."

"HEY, EVERYONE!" the DJ suddenly bellows through his microphone. "That's the Prime Minister's daughter over there! And that's Izzy Williams! Hey, you guys, we love your parents! They are COUPLE GOALS!"

As others approach asking for selfies, Kylie shakes her head at Izzy, gesturing to the small crowd forming around us.

"You see? It's *my* birthday party and it's now all about *you*. Unbelievable."

She turns on her heel and flounces off into the house in a strop, with Jenna and a couple of the other girls running after her.

"Kylie!" Izzy calls, but it's no use. She doesn't turn back.

Looking devastated, Izzy ignores everyone asking for a picture and storms back down the path at the side of the house. I politely agree to take photos with everyone and then thank them for their continued support of my mum, before insisting I have to go and heading off with the security agent.

By the time I climb into the car, Izzy is sitting with her seatbelt on, staring out the window.

"Izzy," I say quietly, "are you—"

"I'm fine," she snaps.

But as we pull out and drive away, I see a tear roll down her cheek.

CHAPTER TEN

"You're in BIG trouble." I shake my head solemnly. "Prepare to be destroyed."

I reach over the chessboard, pick up my knight and take her bishop, knocking it off the board confidently, before clasping my hands together and working out the next move.

My adversary, Rosy, snores loudly, her nose twitching in her sleep. I raise my eyebrows.

"Pretending to be asleep, huh," I say, tutting. "The oldest trick in the book."

I carefully consider the pieces and move Rosy's queen for her.

"Hmm. I wasn't expecting you to do that, Rosy. It's a smart move. A very smart move. You've put a lot of pressure on my knight there, but I suppose you already knew that."

Rosy snores again.

I rest my chin in my hands. Playing chess on my bedroom floor against my dog isn't exactly ideal, but it is excellent practice and if I'm going to play Tony again then I'm going to need to improve. He keeps beating me.

"Ah. That's . . . embarrassing," he said last time, after proclaiming checkmate.

"No, don't be embarrassed," I sighed, wondering how I went so wrong. "You shouldn't apologize, you deserved to win."

"I wasn't talking about me and I wasn't apologizing," he chuckled. "I meant it's embarrassing for you."

I threw a biscuit at his head, but he ducked and Rosy gobbled it up as soon as it hit the floor. I bet him five sweets from the Cabinet Room that I'd beat him next time. And if that means I have to play against Rosy every night on my own, then so be it. I won't be putting up with that smug smile of his much longer.

"Unfortunately for you, Rosy, I am a genius mastermind when it comes to the chessboard," I say, cackling dramatically as I prepare to take the lead in the game. "Watch this. I'm going to—"

Suddenly, my bedroom door swings open and Izzy stands in the doorway looking frazzled. Rosy, abruptly woken by the door slamming against the wall, jumps to her feet and bounds across the room towards our visitor, barging through the chessboard and sending all the pieces flying.

"Nooooooo!" I cry, as the pieces scatter across the floor.

I turn furiously to Izzy. "What are you doing? Don't you *knock?*"

ARGH! Why does she ALWAYS have to ruin things? She is IMPOSSIBLE to like!

I did feel a bit sorry for her after Kylie's party, so was willing to try slightly harder with her. After all, what Kylie did was unfair. I don't know why Izzy would want to be friends with someone who behaves that way. A real friend wouldn't act like that. That's what I told Izzy as we drove away from Kylie's house.

"She should be understanding," I said as Izzy stared bleakly out the window. "She's not being very nice, if you want my opinion."

"I don't want your opinion."

"She must have known you'd find out about her party eventually, through social media or someone telling you," I continued. "She wanted to make you feel left out. If you ask me, you're better off without someone like that. She seems to be good at making people feel small. She made me feel that way and I barely know her."

Izzy didn't say anything. She just continued to stare out the window. I decided to change the subject as obviously she didn't want to talk about it, and proceeded to have a conversation with Hal about the benefits of trampolining. When we got to the trampoline park, Izzy was in such a foul mood she didn't utter one word. She sulked in the background while I chatted to the cheery members of staff, then said that she'd wait in the car with Hal for the rest of the afternoon, refusing to even try out a trampoline.

Since that day she's been even more UNBEARABLE. She's rude to everyone, especially me and Mum, and can't make it through one day without having a strop about *something*.

And now here she is, barging into my bedroom without knocking, causing havoc as usual and destroying my chess game.

"There's no time for knocking. This is too important!" Izzy claims, shutting my door behind her and crouching down to give Rosy a cuddle.

"You've ruined our game! I was about to win!"

She glances at the chess pieces and then back at me, confused.

"Against who?"

"*Whom*," I correct, standing up and putting my hands on my hips. "Against Rosy!"

"You were playing chess against Rosy?"

"Yes!"

She straightens. "You realize Rosy is a dog, right? Don't you need thumbs to move chess pieces? And a basic grasp of the game? I'm going to guess that it's a little more complicated than fetching a tennis ball."

"Technically, I was playing for Rosy," I sigh, irritated that I'm having to explain myself and not sure why I'm bothering.

"So you were playing against . . . yourself? Wow." She grimaces. "That's a bit sad."

"What do you want?" I huff. "You can't storm in here and—"

"It's an emergency. I need to. . ." She hesitates, looking me up and down. "What are those?"

"Excuse me?"

"What are you wearing?"

"Pyjamas!"

"They have dogs on them."

I glance down at my cotton pyjama top and bottoms. "They're wolves, not dogs. And so what?"

"Nothing." She shrugs. "I just didn't have you down as the kind of person who wears pyjamas with cute little dogs all over them to bed, that's all."

"*Wolves*. What did you think I wore to bed?"

"I don't know." She looks thoughtful. "A nightie maybe."

"A *nightie?*"

"Yeah, a frilly white nightie. Like they wore in the Regency period or something."

I narrow my eyes at her. "I may be mature for my age, Izzy, but I'm not a character in a Jane Austen novel. If you must know, these pyjamas were a gift."

"From your mum?"

"From the Queen of Spain."

"Ah."

"The Iberian wolf is native to Spain."

"Cool," she says, looking genuinely interested, which is the first time I've ever seen her drawn in by something I have to say. "Are they dangerous?"

"Yes, Izzy, they're wolves."

"Isn't it kind of weird that Rosy descended from the wolf?" she says as Rosy paws at her leg, whining for attention. "I always find that funny when I think about it. You look at little sausage dogs and tiny cute fluffy dogs and it's like, *how* do you come from the wolf?"

"Yeah, that is weird," I agree. "It's strange to think that. . . Wait. Hang on, why are we talking about wolves? What was the emergency?"

Her eyes widen as she remembers why she barged in here in the first place.

"I think you might need to sit down. Prepare to be shocked."

"I'm sure I can handle whatever you have to say, Izzy."

"I was in Dad's room and I was looking through stuff and—"

"Hang on," I interrupt, holding my hand up. "When you say your dad's room, you actually mean Mum's room. What were you doing going through their things? Were you trying to dye someone's eyebrows again? You know that there are secret service agents in the house, right? I have alerted them to your tricks."

"I wasn't doing anything bad," she insists grumpily. "I was looking for my headphones. And I've said sorry about the eyebrow thing a million times. It was supposed to be funny."

"Why would my mum have your headphones?"

"Not your mum. My dad. He confiscated them."

"Oh. Good for him."

She scowls at me. "The point is, while I was looking for them, I came across something else. Something terrifying."

"A manual on manners?" I offer. "You could do with one of those."

"Pearl, I am being serious," she says desperately, glancing over her shoulder to check the door is closed before lowering her voice to a hushed tone. "Amongst Dad's things, I found a *diamond ring*."

"W-what?"

She nods gravely. "It was in a little box hidden in a shoebox under the bed."

"Are . . . are you sure it wasn't one of Mum's rings?" I ask, my blood running cold. "She has some beautiful jewellery, maybe it was—"

"Pearl, it wasn't one of your mum's. It was an engagement ring."

Oh no. OH NO.

I clasp a hand over my mouth. "Do you think your dad is going to propose with it?"

"No, I think he's going to hula hoop with it." She rolls her eyes. "YES, I think he's going to propose with it!"

"Oh my goodness, *what are we going to do?* If he proposes, she'll say yes!"

"And then Patrice will be my stepmum, and my dad will be your stepdad!"

"And we'll be. . ." I begin. "We'll be. . ."

"*Stepsisters,*" we say in chorus.

We look at each other in pure horror.

"Something HAS to be done to stop this," Izzy says determinedly.

"I agree. But what can we do?"

"We could steal the ring? He can't propose if there isn't a ring to propose with!"

"Yes he can, genius. He can get another one. Or propose without one. And we can't steal a diamond ring, we could go to prison! That's a useless idea."

She puts her hands on her hips. "Do you have a better one, Little Miss Perfect?"

"We could tell them horrible stories about each other?" I suggest, clicking my fingers. "Put them off one another!"

"Oh, so stealing is bad, but lying is no problem. You really are a politician's daughter."

"There's got to be SOMETHING we can come up with together," I say, ignoring her comment and pacing the room. "We have to somehow get them to realize what a terrible idea it would be!"

Izzy's eyes light up. "That's it!"

"What's it?"

"We get them to realize," she says excitedly. "It's so simple! I don't want to be here and I know that you don't want me here."

I shift uncomfortably. It's true, but it seems rude to say it out loud.

"Technically we're on the same side," Izzy continues. "We both want the same thing, so we have to work together to make that happen."

"But how?"

She grins mischievously, stroking her chin like an evil genius in a movie. "Sabotage."

"What?"

"We ruin events, we interrupt meetings, we destroy the house! That's how we win! If we sabotage everything about Downing Street, Dad and I will *have* to move out. Patrice will have no choice but to demand that I leave!"

"And it will go back to being just as it was," I say, letting her words sink in.

"Exactly." Izzy nods vigorously. "You and your mum here, and Dad and I back home, back to the way we were."

"You think this will work?" I bite my lip.

"Of course it will work," Izzy says, before hesitating and giving me a knowing smile. "Especially if you draw up a plan with thorough notes on everything we can do to ruin things."

I brighten. "That's a good idea. We'll need to come up with a good list to pull this off."

"So, we have a deal?" Izzy asks cautiously. "We work together to get me and Dad thrown out the house?"

"We have a deal." I hold out my hand. "Together, we'll work to get you out of here."

She grins, taking my hand and shaking it firmly. "Let the sabotage begin."

CHAPTER ELEVEN

"Welcome back to Battersea, Pearl!"

I step out the car to an enthusiastic greeting from the staff at Battersea Dogs & Cats Home. It's been a couple of months since I was last here meeting everyone for the first time, discussing how I could help promote the amazing work they do.

When Mum was campaigning for Prime Minister, she promised me that if she was elected I could focus on supporting animal welfare, something very important to me. Rosy gets me in a way that no human does and, more than anything, I want to use my platform to help animals get the compassion and respect they deserve. I plan to set up my own animal charity one day.

"It's good to be back," I say, beaming at them. "I'm sorry this was arranged so last minute. Thank you for letting us come at short notice."

"I want to pet all the dogs and cuddle all the cats!" Izzy blurts out excitedly as she slides out the car behind me, followed by Beth. "Show me to the dogs!"

I give her a stern look, but the staff chuckle, thankfully finding her lack of decorum funny.

"I hope you don't mind me bringing Izzy along today," I say to Sarah, the Head of Publicity, who gestures for us to enter the building as Izzy skips along happily next to me.

"It's a pleasure to welcome you both!"

"There is an exciting reason she's accompanying me."

"Oh?" Sarah says, looking intrigued.

"We think it's about time that Rosy got a new canine companion," I say, smiling up at her. "I was wondering if you would consider letting us adopt a dog today? We have brought along all references that you may need and, of course, a confirmation of a home check that states the garden and house are completely secure—"

"Well, I might have guessed that." Sarah laughs. "Probably the most secure house in the country!"

"And you know that Izzy's father Jackson Williams is a world-class dog trainer, so hopefully you'll approve us as potential owners for a dog that needs a forever home."

"That is *wonderful* news," Sarah says, clapping her hands. "We'd love to match you to one of our gorgeous rescues."

"YES!" Izzy punches the air.

"Please do have a seat and we'll get you a tea or coffee," Sarah says. "In the meantime, I'll chat to our trainers to see which of our dogs would be best suited to your lifestyle."

Izzy's face falls. "Can't we go see the dogs?"

"We will in a minute, Izzy," I say through gritted teeth, taking a seat in the waiting room. "You have to be patient. You can't walk in and pick whichever one you want."

Sarah smiles warmly at her. "Don't worry, I won't be long. Keira, please could you get everyone a drink of whatever they want while they wait?"

Beth goes with Keira to help her with the teas, while Izzy paces around the room impatiently and I check my phone for any messages.

"Would you sit down?" I snap after several minutes of Izzy walking back and forth. I bit my tongue for as long as humanly possible, but enough is enough. "You're driving me nuts."

"Fine," she huffs, sitting down.

Somehow, this is worse. She fidgets and shifts about, tapping her chipped neon-blue nails against the plastic chair, kicking the floor with her heels.

"What is WRONG with you?" I cry, scowling at her. "Can't you sit STILL?"

She shakes her head. "Not really. I've never been very patient."

"I can tell."

"At least I don't sit like you."

"What's wrong with the way I sit?"

"You sit like this," she says, happy to give me a demonstration.

Sitting up straight, she keeps her knees together and lifts her chin so high that her head is tilted back and her eyes are looking at the ceiling. She uses her hands to frame her face as though posing for a cheesy photo.

Fully prepared to be insulted, instead I can't help but burst out laughing.

"You look ridiculous! I do not sit like that!"

"You do! And you drink your tea with your pinky in the air, all high and mighty."

"I do NOT!"

She goes back to her slouching, giving me a shrug. "If you say so."

Keira and Beth come back in with the teas and I take mine gratefully, while Izzy launches into a hundred questions about the dogs for poor Keira to answer. Beth and I sit quietly, listening to the interrogation and waiting for Sarah to return.

At one point, Izzy glances over at me as I take a sip

of tea and smiles smugly. I realize that my little finger is raised. I quickly put my mug down as Izzy sniggers into hers.

"We're all set," Sarah announces, peering round the door. "Are you ready to come meet the Battersea dogs?"

"I've never been more ready," Izzy declares, jumping to her feet and spilling her tea down her jeans. "Whoops! Never mind!"

Izzy leads the way with Sarah, asking her lots of questions about the centre and making Sarah laugh with her stories about the naughty dogs that her dad has trained in the past.

"And have you ever had a dog at home?" Sarah asks, pushing through some doors.

"My mum, Catherine, she really wanted one and we were going to get a little rescue dog, but then she got sick. . ." Izzy trails off.

"I'm sure she'd be very proud of you getting a rescue dog now," Sarah says gently. "You're going to give a lucky dog a very happy home."

"Right," Izzy says, collecting herself. "Yeah, she would be proud."

When we were talking about visiting Battersea during our sabotage plotting, Izzy never mentioned that her mum had wanted a rescue. I wonder why she left that detail out. I feel a wave of sympathy for her, and guilt for not being as nice to her as I could have been.

Then I remember that she dyed my eyebrows green and stuck a "LOSER" sign on my back for the whole world to laugh at. The feeling of guilt washes away in an instant.

When we reach the kennels, Izzy can barely contain her excitement, clasping a hand over her mouth and letting out a high-pitched squeak.

"Sarah, about the kind of dog we're specifically after—" I begin, prompting Izzy to remember why we decided to come here in the first place.

"Oh yes," she says, taking over. "We want a really mischievous one. As you know, my dad can train any dog, so it doesn't matter if they're naughty. In fact, I think a naughty dog would suit me best. Preferably a very scruffy-looking dog. Very, very scruffy. Dirty almost. A dog that might leave mud all over cream carpets and posh hallways."

Sarah looks surprised at such a request. "All right, I'll have a think."

She introduces us to the dogs one by one and stands back to let us admire them and shower them in the attention they deserve. The ones who are confident enough to meet us bark in joy and lick our faces and roll over so we can rub their bellies. It's hard not to take all of them home and I wonder whether it might be OK to squeeze around fifty or so dogs into Downing Street. It seems IMPOSSIBLE to choose just one. They all deserve a happy home.

Izzy seems to be having the same dilemma, sitting down on the ground with them and falling in love with each dog that covers her in licks. Luckily, we have Sarah to help us make a decision.

"I think I may have a dog that fits your … uh … specifications," she says, sharing a look with one of the trainers. "Come with me."

Izzy clambers to her feet and brushes the dust off her jeans, and we follow Sarah down to an end kennel in anticipation.

"Pearl and Izzy," Sarah begins, opening the kennel door, "I'd like you to meet Bugsy."

Bugsy is a total SCRUFFBALL. A complete mix of breeds, he's a little bigger than Rosy, with grey, scraggly fur, and so much energy he's bouncing off the walls, a blur of grey floof as he zips past. He is so excited to see us that he takes a running jump, leaping at Izzy's legs with such enthusiasm that he reflects off, doing a bizarre somersault before flying towards me. His tongue lolls out, slobber flies everywhere and his large bedraggled ears flap about as he spins around in manic circles.

"As you can see, he's . . . well, he matches what you just mentioned," Sarah says, wincing as he crashes into the wall and then carries on running around as though nothing's happened. "He's a little unkempt, and he'd need a lot of training, but he's very affectionate. No aggression in him. The thing is, I'm not sure he wouldn't cause a bit of chaos in such an important house. There are some other dogs that you should meet, ones that might be more—"

"No need, Sarah," Izzy says, watching Bugsy affectionately as he barks at a fly and then tries to chase it, slipping and sliding across the floor after it, before suddenly coming to a halt in order to have a good scratch, hair moulting in a cloud around him.

Izzy looks at me and I give a nod in solidarity. Bugsy howls at his bed.

"He's bonkers," Beth notes, watching him wide-eyed.

"He's chaotic," Sarah sighs.

"He's impossible," the trainer says.

"He's *perfect*," I declare, sharing a grin with Izzy. "We'll take him."

Mum is not happy. In fact, it would be fair to say she's furious. It's exactly how we planned.

"What on EARTH were you thinking?" she cries as

Bugsy runs around the house, Izzy chasing after him in delight.

Rosy is standing at my feet, watching Bugsy race around. She is wary of a new dog, but her tail wags as though she's tempted to join in.

"Pearl! Explain yourself at once!" Mum demands.

"Sorry, Mum?" I say, feigning confusion. "Explain what exactly?"

"Why you and— AHHHHHH!"

She dodges out the way as Bugsy zooms past her, Izzy almost falling over Maya in hot pursuit. Rosy can't hold back any longer. Her old instincts kick in and she bolts after Izzy, joining in on the chase.

"Why you and Izzy decided to get a dog without my permission!" Mum continues, her eyes wide with horror as Bugsy loses his footing and does several forward rolls across the floor, crashing into the bottom of the stairs. He shakes his head and then barks happily, leaping upstairs, desperate to explore his new home. Rosy barks along with him, overtaking him on the stairs – to show him around, I assume.

"I thought you'd be happy," I say calmly.

"*Happy?*"

"Yes. About Izzy and I doing something together. Bonding. You encouraged us to do that, didn't you?"

"Well, yes, but couldn't you have—"

"And it's important to lead by example, Mum, you taught me that. Giving a rescue a loving home will encourage others to do the same. These dogs deserve families, don't you agree?"

"Of course, but—"

"Exactly."

"That dog is a ... a MENACE!" she declares, watching Bugsy come tumbling back down the stairs with Rosy while Izzy slides down the bannister after them. "Izzy! Please don't do that!"

"Do what, Patrice?" Izzy asks innocently, sliding off the end and landing with a loud thump on the floor.

"That bannister is very— OH MY GOODNESS!" Mum gasps as she sees Bugsy cock his leg on a policeman's leg. "STOP THAT DOG!"

The policeman jumps back a touch too late, his trousers receiving an unfortunate splash. Bugsy barks and then runs off to cause chaos in the kitchen. We hear a loud crash and a scream from the chef. Doors from all the rooms downstairs creak open as ministers and staff peer out, eager to see what is going on.

"So nice of Izzy to give Bugsy a loving home," I say cheerily as Mum buries her head in her hands. "Anyway, I'd better go upstairs and prepare for my music lesson with Izzy. See you!"

"Wait, music lesson with Izzy? What do you mean?" Mum calls out behind me as I run up the stairs, pretending not to hear her.

Minutes later, Izzy joins me in the master bedroom carrying her speakers, as we'd planned. She places them on Mum's dressing table. The master bedroom is directly above the Cabinet Room and nearest the stairs. We're going for maximum effect.

"Where are the dogs?" I ask, after reminding her to leave the door wide open.

"Beth and Gabrielle are trying to get them out of the pantry," she informs me. "Apparently Bugsy found the crisps stash."

"Perfect. So, are you ready to give me a music lesson?"

"Yes, I am." She grins. "Your education is about to begin."

She scrolls down her phone and picks a song, pressing play. It blares out the speakers as she turns up the volume as high as it can go. I cover my ears, grimacing. It sounds AWFUL.

She says something, but I can't hear her above the noise.

"WHAT DID YOU SAY?" I yell.

"THIS IS PUNK ROCK!" she shouts back. "WHAT DO YOU THINK?"

"THIS IS THE WORST SONG I'VE EVER HEARD!"

"YOU'LL LOVE IT!"

"HOW DO YOU LISTEN TO THIS? IT DOESN'T EVEN HAVE A TUNE!"

"IT HAS ATTITUDE! IT HAS EMOTION! YOU NEED TO DANCE!"

"I NEED TO WHAT?"

"YOU NEED TO DANCE!" she bellows. "I'LL SHOW YOU."

She begins jumping up and down, throwing her arms around wildly in the air.

I shake my head at her. "I CAN'T DO THAT!"

"WHY NOT? EVERYONE CAN! GO ON, TRY!"

As she continues bouncing around the room, I attempt a little bop, heat rising to my cheeks in embarrassment.

"DON'T WORRY ABOUT WHAT YOU LOOK LIKE!" she instructs. "JUST LET GO!"

I try my best to do as she says, nodding my head a bit more, swaying a bit more. I recoil when she leaps towards me, but she doesn't let me get away with it, grabbing my hands and encouraging me to follow her lead.

"JUMP! JUMP! STOMP THOSE FEET!"

I start jumping along with her.

"THAT'S IT! YOU'RE DOING IT! MORE, MORE!"

Soon, I'm jumping as high as her and unable to stop laughing, thinking about how silly this is. I'm jumping around to a horrible, screeching, thumping song.

But it's also kind of *fun*.

We get so into it, neither of us notices Mum, Jackson, grumpy Sebastian and several other people standing in the doorway yelling at us, until Jackson stomps across to Izzy's phone on the dressing table and turns the music off, his expression thunderous.

The room falls into silence as Izzy and I catch our breath.

"Hey!" Izzy says, folding her arms. "Why did you turn our music off?"

"*Pearl*," Mum says to me, aghast. "What are you *doing*?"

"Izzy's giving me a music lesson," I say with a shrug, Izzy nodding in agreement. "I'm learning how songs have attitude."

"The music has to be loud for this kind of lesson," Izzy explains innocently. "I always played music this loud at home and I've never had any complaints before. The thing is, any quieter and I can't really hear it. What did you think of the genre? Are you a fan of punk rock, Patrice? I'm a HUGE fan."

Mum looks aghast. She has no idea how to reply.

"Do you know how many meetings you've DISTURBED?" Sebastian yells, looking as though he might explode with anger. "This cannot happen AGAIN!"

With that, he turns on his heel and stomps away down the stairs. Mum watches him go, looking pained.

"He's technically not allowed up here," I point out to her. "You should remind him that this is private quarters. He's not allowed to shout at me either."

"He has every right to be mad at you," Mum says, hands on her hips. "First the dog, now this! I don't know what has got into you, Pearl, but consider yourself grounded for the next two days."

"You too, Izzy," Jackson says sternly. "I'm so disappointed in you. Remember where you are. I'm confiscating your phone."

"I have hugely important meetings this afternoon. I expect no more trouble from either of you," Mum says, her eyes scanning from me to Izzy and back to me again. "We'll talk about this tonight."

Neither Izzy nor I offer an apology, stubbornly remaining silent as Mum and Jackson leave the room, shaking their heads at us.

"What a shame," Izzy sighs, once they're safely downstairs and out of earshot. "Looks like I've caused a LOT of trouble at Downing Street today."

"Looks like you have."

"Want to help me cause some more?"

I reach into my pocket and happily pass her my phone to connect to the speakers. "Yes, Izzy. I do. Turn the volume up as high as it goes."

CHAPTER TWELVE

I've discovered I'm not very good at rollerblading.

Izzy can't believe I've never tried it before. She's REALLY good at it.

"I need to read the instructions," I insist, clinging to the bannister at the bottom of the stairs, my legs slipping around beneath me like Bambi walking on ice.

"What do you mean?" Izzy replies, gliding elegantly past me, the shiny floors of the hall perfect for the activity. "There aren't any instructions."

"There's no manual? Surely one comes with the rollerblades."

"Um, no," she says, looking at me as though I'm deranged. "You learn as you go."

"That can't be right. Did you lose the instruction manual and now you're making this up?"

"Pearl, there is no instruction manual. It's like riding

a bike. Instructions only get you so far, you have to learn by doing it. Let go of the bannister and give it a try. I'll teach you."

I gulp, slowly loosening my grip only for my feet to roll out underneath me. I clutch the bannister again for dear life before I fall.

"No, no, no." I shake my head. "I have to take these off."

Izzy comes to a stop in front of me and puts her hands on her hips. "Not a natural sportsperson, eh?"

"Excuse me, I am very much a natural sportsperson," I argue, desperately trying to keep my balance, my helmet knocking against the rails of the bannister as I slide about. "It simply depends on the sport."

"Oh yeah? Which one?"

"Well. Chess, for one—"

"Chess is not a sport."

"—and I'm also not bad at bowling—"

"Are you kidding me?"

"—and I had a natural flair for snooker when I tried it once."

"OK, stop, you're embarrassing yourself." She laughs, receiving a sharp glare from me. "None of those sports involve . . . you know . . . moving."

"That's not true! You have to walk up to a bowling

alley! And you know I do yoga and my instructor says I'm a natural at—"

"Pearl, let go of the bannister."

"No."

She sighs. "Even if you fall, you're wearing knee and elbow pads, and a helmet. It won't hurt. Much. The reason you're so wobbly is because you're leaning on the bannister. You have to try to find your own balance. Here."

She holds out her hands. I look at them.

"What?"

"Take my hands," she insists.

"HA!" I snort. "No chance. You'll, no doubt, pull me forwards so I land flat on my face and you'll film it and put it up online."

"I promise I won't do that. As funny as that would be. I'm actually planning on helping you."

I narrow my eyes at her. "How do I know if I can trust you? You hate me."

"I don't know," she says with a shrug, before lowering her voice. "We're working together, right? We're on the same team. You falling over on rollerblades doesn't exactly help my cause. But us skating around the house together causing havoc, that works for me." She pauses. "And I don't hate you."

"You dyed my eyebrows green."

"Are you ever going to get over that?"

"No."

"OK." She looks at me expectantly, wiggling her fingers. "Come on, Pearl. Take my hands. I won't let you fall. Do as I say – stay on top of the wheels, don't let your ankles lean either way, just keep them straight. Make sure your toes are pointing straight ahead."

Part of me wants to give up, sit back down on the bottom step and take these stupid things off my feet. But the other part of me is aware that the door custodian and a policeman on guard, despite pretending not to take any notice of what's going on, are smiling to themselves. If I don't give this a try, I'll look pathetic.

At least Rosy and Bugsy aren't here to mock me too. We've left them outside for a training session with a very stressed-out Jackson. Apparently, Bugsy has reignited Rosy's love of digging holes in the rose garden.

I take a deep breath and go through everything Izzy just said. I gently push myself away from the bannister so that I'm standing on top of the wheels, rather than leaning my feet in. I carefully let go of the bannister with one hand and place that hand in Izzy's. When I feel steady, I very slowly let go with the other hand and take her free one.

"What now?" I squeak.

"Get used to balancing on your own. Then we'll think about moving. You have to let go of my hands first. You've got this far, you can definitely do the next step."

"OK. You're right."

She loosens her grip and I let her pull her hands away.

"Pearl! You did it!" She smiles, moving backwards to get a good look at me as I stand with my arms outstretched, keeping my balance like a frozen scarecrow. "You're officially balancing on rollerblades!"

I beam at her. "Cool!"

"Guess I was wrong about you not being a natural sportsperson."

"Yes, you were," I say, frightened to move a muscle.

She laughs and the policeman catches my eye and gives me a small, silent clap. Recently I've met ambassadors, given awards, opened exhibitions. But standing on rollerblades on my own feels like my greatest achievement.

The policeman's encouragement and Izzy's guidance give me a boost of confidence I didn't realize I had. By the end of the day, I'm moving unsteadily around the hallway, with only a few minor bumps and falls.

And by the end of the week, Izzy and I are rollerblading around the house, whooping and cheering as we dodge ministers on their way to meetings, narrowly avoiding crashes with household staff and bursting into rooms, skating round meeting tables and zooming out again before anyone has the chance to yell at us.

"We need to have a little talk before tonight."

Mum shuts my bedroom door behind her, clearing her throat and marching into the middle of the room. I am at my dressing table fiddling with the clasp of my bracelet, while Rosy snoozes soundly on my bed. Now that she spends all day playing with Bugsy, by the evenings she's worn out.

"What's up, Mum?"

"This evening is very important."

"I know," I say, frowning in concentration as I finally manage to shut the clasp safely. "It's not every day you have dinner with the Queen, the Duke and Duchess of Cornwall AND the Duke and Duchess of Cambridge."

"I want to make sure that you don't have anything up your sleeve."

I blink at her innocently. "What do you mean?"

"It hasn't gone unnoticed that there has been a slight shift in your behaviour recently. The disruption and chaos of the household has gone up a few notches in recent weeks."

"I haven't noticed anything. Is this to do with sneaking sweets from the Cabinet Room? Because Tony said that was OK."

"It's a little more than a few sweets going missing. I'm not sure if you saw it online, but apparently Sebastian noticed the paparazzi laughing when he left yesterday, and when he walked through his front door he realized that there had been a note stuck to his back the whole time that read 'GRUMPYHEAD'. You wouldn't know anything about that, would you?"

I try not to laugh, keeping my eyes on the floor as I shake my head.

My idea. Genius.

"This morning," she continues calmly, "I went into an education meeting only to find that the important notes painstakingly put together by Gabrielle in my folder had been replaced by a bunch of silly drawings of Bugsy as Prime Minister."

Izzy's idea. Also genius.

"And let us not forget the incident with the house intercom system the other day. Somehow the person in charge of it was locked out of the room, while two people blew raspberries and giggled through the speakers of Downing Street during a presidential visit."

A team effort. Joint genius.

"Very creative," I say, reaching for my perfume and giving my wrists a spritz. "Don't you think?"

"Yes, and I'm sure it was very funny for you, but it certainly was not for me."

"Mum, you're the one who keeps grounding us. Izzy and I are stuck here together, so we have to find ways to entertain ourselves. Before Izzy came along, I was happy with a book, or a quiet game of chess with Rosy, but with her here, it makes a lot more sense to dance around to music or learn how to rollerblade. Have you ever tried it?"

"Pearl, I know what you're doing. You and Izzy are in it together."

I avoid looking at her. I know she's giving me that terrifying stare of hers that has brought world leaders to their knees, so I keep busying myself with bits and bobs on the dressing table.

"We're not doing anything, Mum. As you know, Izzy and I can't stand each other."

She inhales deeply and as she exhales, she marches back across the room.

"Tonight has to go well, Pearl," Mum says in a softer tone. "I can't have any more bad press."

I feel a pang of guilt. That is the only downside to mine and Izzy's plan, and something I didn't completely think through when we embarked on our sabotage mission. A lot of the headlines about Mum and the government have been very negative or mocking recently, mostly prompted by whatever chaos we've caused. People are asking, if Mum can't control her household or her family, how can she possibly keep control of the country? I know her popularity has been dipping. . .

But I comfort myself with the knowledge that we're so close to breaking point. They can't put up with this much longer. Just a few more tricks and Izzy and Jackson will HAVE to move out. As soon as that happens, everything will go back to normal and Mum will be back on track. It's for her own good that our plan works.

And that means tonight has to go wrong.

I am absolutely TERRIFIED.

It's one thing *talking* about ruining dinner with the Queen, it's another to actually go through with it. To be completely honest, if it wasn't for Izzy I couldn't do it. Izzy has more flaws than anyone I know: she's very loud, rude, annoyingly brash and has as much elegance as a walrus, but I have to give it to her, the girl has guts.

I'm not entirely sure about the plan for this evening, I only know that there is one. We need Mum to realize that it is impossible for anything to go smoothly when Izzy and Jackson live here, including dinners with royalty.

Hosting the royal family at Downing Street has been in the diary for a while, and the invitation was extended to include Jackson and Izzy when they first moved in. Mum clearly regrets this now but she can't tell them not to come at this stage. She made sure that Rosy and Bugsy were excluded, shut safely upstairs under the watch of one of Jackson's trainer contacts. Mum and Jackson refused to trust Izzy and me to be in charge of that side of things.

"What exactly do we do?" I asked Izzy when she first suggested we ruin the evening.

"I can't tell you," Izzy replied haughtily.

"Why not?" I asked, a little put out. "We're in this together, aren't we?"

"Yes, but you won't like it. You'll be all ... *you* about it."

"What does that mean?"

"Nothing! Just, you're quite a ... tense person. And this plan involves being relaxed. Especially when it comes to –" she put on a mock-posh voice, waving her hands in the air with a flourish – "*etiquette*. Trust me, I'm doing you a favour by not warning you about it. You simply have to promise that you'll go along with everything when it starts."

"How will I know when it starts?"

"Oh, you'll know."

"It isn't anything that's going to get us imprisoned for treason, is it?"

She hesitated, looking thoughtful. "I don't *think* so."

Not very comforting.

After we've gone through the nerve-racking process of welcoming the royal family to Downing Street, standing outside for a million photos and then showing them to the formal dining room, I take my seat at the dining table with butterflies flitting about in my stomach.

The Queen is sat at the top of the table next to Mum and they're deep in conversation by the time starters are served, while Jackson chats away next to them with the Duke and Duchess of Cornwall. The Duke and Duchess of Cambridge are at my end, and they're so nice and attentive that I almost forget my nerves as they chat and laugh like we're all old friends. I have to keep reminding myself they're royalty.

Izzy is noticeably quiet and I keep trying to catch her eye, but she's purposefully avoiding looking in my direction. Disrupting tonight's dinner seemed like a good idea, but now we're here I wish we'd never considered it. I hope she doesn't go too far. If only I knew what she had planned. Not knowing what's about to happen is MUCH worse. *What has she got up her sleeve?*

By the time mains are served, I wonder whether she's bottled it. I wouldn't be surprised if she has; it is a BIG deal to try to sabotage an evening with royalty, and I imagine she would have already gone ahead with it if she was going to do it.

I start to relax, digging into the delicious parsley and garlic risotto, served with mushrooms in a truffle and hazelnut sauce. I'm halfway through when I turn to the Duke of Cambridge cheerily, putting my fork down to take a sip of homemade lemonade.

"And what is the food like at Buckingham Palace?" I begin. "I've always wondered if—"

SPLAT!!

The room instantly falls into shocked silence. I look down at my Chanel blouse to see risotto dripping into my lap from where it struck me, in the middle of the pretty black bow at the neckline. I lift my eyes to look at Izzy sitting directly across from me, her spoon held aloft.

"Oopsie," she says breezily.

The Duke and Duchess of Cambridge are frozen in shock, their mouths wide open. Mum looks absolutely appalled. Jackson buries his head in his hands. The Duke and Duchess of Cornwall look completely at a loss, blinking at me in confusion.

The Queen, however, barely flinches. She seems mildly amused at this turn of events.

"*Izzy!*" I hiss, barely able to speak I'm so angry. "What are you DOING?"

"My hand slipped." She shrugs. "Guess you'll just have to *go with it.*"

She glances down pointedly at my half-eaten risotto and then back up at me, her eyes wide with meaning. She gives me a sharp, encouraging nod.

Oh. Oh no. No, no, no. This can't be her plan. It CAN'T be.

Well, I won't do it. I won't throw any food across the table in front of THE QUEEN. Has Izzy completely lost her mind?! Does she really think that this is the best way to—

SPLAT!!

"ARGH!" I cry out as a truffle-soaked mushroom hits me square in the forehead.

"Whoops," Izzy sighs, waving her fork at me. "Slipped again."

How dare she?! The Chanel is one thing, but now she's aiming for MY FACE! That's it. She's asked for it. *She wants to mess with me?* SHE WANTS TO MESS WITH ME?!

"Isabella!" Jackson shouts, jumping to his feet.

"I'm so sorry, Your Majesty," Mum says hurriedly. "I'm so, so sorry. I promise it—"

SPLAT!!

Mwahahaha. I sit back smugly as creamy risotto slides down Izzy's nose. She reaches for a napkin, wiping her face. For someone who's not a sportsperson, I sure do have good aim. Well, that will teach her.

"PEARL!" Mum snaps furiously.

"She started it!" I argue.

SPLAT!!

Everyone gasps in unison. Izzy sent a spoonful of risotto flying across the table, but instead of hitting me, it's landed in the middle of the Duke of Cambridge's chest. He blinks down at his ruined blue shirt.

"*Oh my god,*" Mum whispers, her hands over her mouth. "What have you done?"

SPLAT!!

This time the Duke of Cambridge is struck with a mushroom right on the head. And it didn't come from Izzy's direction. We all turn to look at the culprit in disbelief.

"I do *love* a good food fight," the Queen declares.

"Excellent aim, Your Majesty!" Izzy exclaims, giving her an enthusiastic round of applause. The Queen nods gratefully.

Bursting out laughing, the Duke of Cambridge spoons some risotto up and lobs it at his wife. She ducks just in time and it hits the wall behind her. As he apologises profusely to Mum about the wallpaper, the Duchess of Cambridge determinedly retaliates, sending a spoonful of her food flying across the table. Chuckling heartily, the Duke of Cornwall decides to get in on the action, but his wife gets in before him, hitting him in the jaw with a mushroom.

The dining room descends into excitable chaos. Food is being thrown all over the place. The Queen's security team by the door look baffled, prepared to step in but deciding not to when they see the Queen delightedly using her spoon as a makeshift catapult, her risotto soaring through the air at her chosen victims as she cries, "Take that!" before ducking swiftly when food comes back her way.

By the time the plates are empty, everyone but the Queen is covered in food. She was by far the best at the game. Realizing that the food fight has come to a natural end, the waiters leap into action, offering napkins and damp towels for us to clean up with. We stand around the table, risotto dripping down our faces and clothes, big beaming smiles on all our faces.

Well. Almost all.

Mum is not smiling. She's not even close to smiling. Collecting herself, she gestures for the royal family to take their seats.

"Now that's over," she says through gritted teeth, "dessert, anyone?"

CHAPTER THIRTEEN

I dozily open my eyes, squinting into blinding torchlight.

"AHHHH!" I scream, covering my face with my arms.

"It's me!" Izzy whispers, shushing me. "It's only me!"

"What are you doing in my room?" I hiss at her, turning on my bedside light and rubbing my eyes. "You never knock! Why aren't you asleep?"

"Because I only went to bed about half an hour ago?" she says, as though it's a strange question for me to ask.

She hops up on to the end of my bed, turning her phone light off. Bugsy, who has followed her in, jumps up to lie next to Rosy and nip at her ears playfully.

"Still rocking those wolf pyjamas I see," Izzy comments.

"Oh, like yours are so fabulous?"

She's wearing a black T-shirt much too big for her – maybe an old one of her dad's – and some pyjama bottoms that look as though they were once blue but have been washed so many times over the years they've faded to grey.

"These are comfy," she says with a shrug. "Sorry for waking you. You fall asleep quickly."

"I have a sleep meditation app and lavender oil mist spray for my pillows."

"Of course you do. Is there anything you do that's not, you know, for grandmas?"

"All I can say to that, Izzy, is that I fall asleep in no time while here you are, wide awake. Clearly, me and the grandmas are on to something."

She smiles. "Right. Anyway, I wanted to check you're OK after tonight. Did Patrice tell you off big time?"

"She didn't say much," I tell her, yawning. "I think she'll want to talk to us tomorrow. What did your dad say?"

"That I'm grounded for ever." She pulls up the end of my duvet and sticks her feet under to keep them warm while we chat. "He said he was really disappointed in me."

"That's the worst. When they're disappointed rather than angry. Mum always plays that card on me."

"Before I came along and we started our mission, I can't picture her ever being disappointed in you." She frowns. "You're, like, the perfect daughter. You and your mum have the best relationship."

"I'm definitely not the perfect daughter," I admit, plumping up the pillow behind me and sitting up. "I have to try so hard to get things right. During Mum's campaign I made loads of mistakes."

"Like what?"

"Once a reporter asked me if I thought Mum was going to be a better leader of the UK than the one at the time. I said something like, 'Yeah, she's going to be WAY better.' Next day there was a bunch of stuff online about me snubbing the Prime Minister. Mum had to make some phone calls to explain. I felt so bad, I thought I might have ruined Mum's chances. I learnt to be careful of what I say to people. Anyone can twist anything if they want to. Mum was pretty disappointed in me that day."

"That's horrible. Must be hard to know who to trust."

"I can trust Rosy." I pat her head and she rolls on to her back for me to rub her belly. Bugsy follows suit.

"I get in trouble with Dad a lot," Izzy says suddenly, her forehead creased. "I think he doesn't really know how to handle me since Mum died. I used to be quite good at school, but it's hard to concentrate on stuff when you're feeling sad."

"You must miss her."

"Yeah." She sighs. "Do you miss your dad?"

"I don't think so. I never knew him, not properly. He left when I was really young. Sometimes I think I can remember him, but then I'm not sure if I'm making it up. If that makes sense."

"I have the same. I'm not sure if all my memories of Mum from when I was little are real, or whether I've seen photos and think I can remember those specific moments."

"Was she good with animals?" I ask curiously, tickling Bugsy's belly and making Rosy jealous.

"Yeah, she wasn't quite so crazy about them as Dad is, but I guess not many people are." Izzy laughs. "She was really into music and stuff. She took me to my first ever concert. She was an amazing cook, too."

"She probably wouldn't have been too pleased with the food fight tonight, then."

"Nah, she would have loved it." Izzy grins. "She was really fun and silly. She would have laughed her head off."

"She sounds cool."

"She was."

We both fall silent.

"Anyway, I should go back to bed," Izzy says eventually. "Sorry again for waking you. I know tonight went as we wanted it to, but I wanted to make sure you weren't in too much trouble when it was all my idea."

I nod as she hops down from the bed. "Thanks for checking."

"Come on, Bugsy, let's go," she says, patting her leg. Bugsy jumps down, padding across the floor towards her. "Night, Pearl."

"Wait a second."

She stops at the door. "Yeah?"

"Here, try this." I grab a bottle from my bedside table and throw it to her.

She catches it, reads the label and raises her eyebrows. "Lavender oil mist. Seriously? I'm not a hundred and eight years old."

"Give it a chance." I snuggle back down into my pillows with a smile and turn off my light. "Sometimes things can surprise you."

IZZY'S BLOG

The plan is working.

Dad is so stressed, there's no way he can put up with this much longer. I've never seen him so worked up before, even when he's attempted to train the naughtiest dogs in the world. He's always so calm and sure of himself, ready for the challenge, but not right now. The other day, I actually saw him pull some of his hair out as he yelled at me.

It was kind of gross.

And Patrice is in a bad way. I can tell she absolutely hates having me here right now, even though she's trying to make out like everything is under control. But she must be at breaking point. I am basically ruining her life. For her own good, of course.

I have to admit I'm impressed with how she's handled it. The Sebastian guy, that serious MP who is always frowning, explodes at me at least once a day, but Patrice is more in control of her emotions and seems more interested in figuring me out than yelling at me.

Like the day after dinner with the Queen, she put some time aside specially to come chat to me. I get why she would be angry, even though it was the best food fight of all time. I overheard the Queen saying to Patrice when she left that she had had a VERY fun evening.

Still, it made sense that I wouldn't be in Patrice's good books. But it turned out that she didn't want to shout at me and tell me off or whatever, instead she "just wanted to talk".

She came up to my room with a tub of ice cream and two spoons. It was my favourite flavour too, strawberry. She said that Dad had told her that.

She kind of caught me off guard. Normally I'd be rude to her, but I thought it was nice that she had bothered to ask Dad what my favourite flavour might be. Then I realized that if she's half as organized as her bonkers daughter then that makes total sense. She probably made notes on me before we met. Still. It was a small gesture that meant a lot, I guess.

Anyway, I fully expected her to reiterate that I was grounded for eternity or for her to take my phone or something as punishment, but instead she asked me how I was settling in. She said she appreciated it must have been a huge move for me and everything must be so overwhelming and difficult.

She wanted me to know that even though she's busy being the Prime Minister, she's always there if I want to talk, even if she's not my favourite person.

Which is nice. I wasn't expecting that.

But, whatever, the point is, it doesn't matter. My dad and I don't belong here and it's important that I stick to the plan and get kicked out of here asap. I can't let Patrice being nice distract me from my goal.

Yeah, the sabotage is not great for Patrice and Dad but one day they'll thank us.

They'll realize that Pearl and I did them a HUGE favour. Because this dysfunctional family could NEVER work. Not in a million years. Pearl and I are WAY too different. We clash. It's a nightmare. Simple.

Although...

OK, so I don't like saying this, and I would only write this here where no one will ever read it – (IF YOU'RE READING THIS AND YOU'RE NOT ME, GO AWAY!) – but it has been a little bit fun working with Pearl on this whole sabotage thing.

A TINY bit.

She's maybe not quite so strait-laced as I thought. When she wants to be, she can be quite funny. When she lets go a little and is just herself, rather than The-Daughter-Of-The-Prime-Minister.

For example, last night she knocked on my door and asked if I wanted to watch a movie. I was like, "Duh, NO" after the last experience, but she said she promised she wouldn't ask so many questions if I promised not to throw posh popcorn at her head. (I didn't realize she knew it was me.)

We watched a silly comedy (she let me choose)

with Rosy and Bugsy curled up next to us, and it was kind of cool. Whenever I've watched films with friends in the past, I've never been the one to choose the movie. Kylie always chose and then Jenna and I would agree. That's how most things worked, to be honest.

I've learnt that Pearl has got a really weird laugh. It's kind of infectious. So when she laughs at something, I laugh because her laugh is so stupid.

I think I also may have judged her style too quickly. Now that I've given her some tips on how to accessorize and make some of her posh dresses a bit more casual with a leather jacket or whatever, she looks miles better.

She actually let me borrow a designer skirt and top last week. At first I laughed in her face when she asked if I wanted to look through her wardrobe, but instead of being all rude back to me, she rolled her eyes, grabbed my arm and dragged me into her room, forcing me to try stuff on.

You know what? I looked good. Once I put my own spin on it, of course.

And it was quite fun sitting down at the weekend with her and Tony over a board game. The rules were stupidly complicated and the whole game was basically impossible, but Pearl was quite patient, advising me on what moves to make and which cards to choose.

"Who taught you to play this?" I asked her.

"Mum did."

"How come I'm so bad at it?"

"You're not. I was much worse when I started. You'll get the hang of it. You need to concentrate. You're easily distracted."

"Can I have that biscuit or are you going to eat it?"

"You can have it."

"Thanks. Wait. I'm lost. What happens now? Is it my move?"

"No, Izzy, you just won."

Yeah, that's right. I won! I never win anything! I was so proud of myself that I did a dance around the room and made Tony laugh. Pearl tried not to laugh, but that infectious giggle/snort of hers came out eventually when I wiggled my bum around. Then we played again and this time Pearl didn't help me so much, because I told her I didn't need help because HELLO I was the reigning champion, and then I came last.

But still. I'm going to practise with Bugsy and beat her next time.

So yeah, Pearl isn't as bad as I thought. It can't be easy being Patrice's daughter. The expectation, the pressure, people judging you all the time. And she's had to do it all by herself. Must be tough.

Anyway. What was I saying? Oh yeah. The plan is working.

I'll be out of here and back to my old life in no time.

CHAPTER FOURTEEN

NO-SHOW PATRICE! FIRST SECRETARY OF STATE STEPS UP!

Family drama causes Patrice Francis to miss yet ANOTHER conference as Sebastian Webber takes the lead again.

COULD SERIOUS SEBASTIAN STEAL THE TOP JOB?

Rumours of a coup as MPs turn on PM and line up Sebastian Webber to replace her.

ALL EYES ON YOU, PM!

Patrice Francis due to give important speech at the Lord Mayor's Banquet tonight!

OPINION PIECE: THE PM
CANNOT HANDLE HER
HOUSEHOLD. HOW CAN WE
TRUST HER TO PUT HER
COUNTRY FIRST?

Wesley Waffle questions the Prime Minister's
lack of loyalty.

The Lord Mayor's Banquet is a really important event in the Prime Minister's calendar. It's a fancy black-tie dinner held at Mansion House in London, which is a huge, grand building, and the dinner is attended by all the senior government figures. At the end of the dinner, Mum is giving a big speech that she's been working on for a long time with her best advisers.

She has asked Jackson to accompany her in the car to the banquet, instead of me. I'm with Izzy in another one following behind. It's the first time she's wanted Jackson in the car with her, and not me, on the way to an event like this one. I'm a bit put out by it.

"I don't think it means anything. She doesn't want to hurt your feelings," Izzy says with a shrug, pulling at the neck of her dress. "It makes sense for her and Dad to go in one car and us in another. They're dating."

"Stop tugging at your dress," I huff, reaching over to slap her hand down. "You'll tear it! The material is very delicate."

"You mean clingy," she retorts, narrowing her eyes at me. "Why do I have to wear this thing anyway? I never wear stuff like this."

"It's a black-tie event. Don't you think it's nice to dress up once in a while? I think you look really lovely."

"You're only saying that because *you* picked the dress. If I'd had my way—"

"If you'd had your way, Izzy, you'd be arriving at the banquet wearing ripped jeans and a grubby old T-shirt." I finish her sentence with a knowing smile.

"None of my T-shirts are grubby. At least I can breathe in them," she says defensively, before slumping back in her seat. "And I meant what I said before, I don't think it means anything that Patrice asked Dad to go with her. She probably wants to run through her speech or whatever. You shouldn't read into it. You always do that."

I frown. "Always do what?"

"Read into things. You're an overthinker."

"No, I'm not!" I retort, even though I know she's right. "And it's better than not thinking about anything.

You never look before you leap. If you'd just waited a few minutes for Chef to come help us the other day before you attempted to flambé pancakes, like I said we should, we wouldn't have set fire to the kitchen and Mum wouldn't have missed that conference!"

"If you'd grabbed the fire extinguisher and aimed it at the pan like *I* said, instead of reading the instructions on the side of it for about half an hour, the fire would have been put out straight away!"

"Well if *you* had—"

"We're here!" Beth trills from the front seat, swivelling round to look at us. We slowly pull up to the steps of Mansion House where a crowd of paparazzi awaits the arriving guests. "Promise me you'll be on your best behaviour tonight, girls? It's none of my business, but I know how important it is to Patrice."

"Don't worry," I assure her, nervously smoothing a crinkle from the skirt of my dress. "We won't cause any trouble tonight. Will we, Izzy?"

She gives a salute. "You won't even know we're here."

Beth gets out along with our driver and we wait a few moments as he comes round to open our door.

"Remember our pact about tonight," I whisper to Izzy hurriedly.

"Relax, Pearl! I already promised nothing will go

wrong."

I breathe a sigh of relief at her sincerity. The plan to get Izzy and Jackson kicked out is working perfectly, but Mum has had so much bad press recently, there are rumours that she might lose her job and grumpy Sebastian will take over. And the only reason she's got bad press is because Izzy and I have been doing everything in our power to cause trouble, which has led to Mum missing events or speeches where people are counting on her. In no way was our family sabotage meant to lead to Mum losing her job.

So, we made a pact: nothing goes wrong tonight. Mum will make her speech, win everyone over once again, and everything will be fine.

The car door swings open and I step out to a flurry of camera flashes and cries from the reporters. I smile sweetly on the red carpet, stopping to pose in my purple, floor-length gown by a new British designer. I'm wearing a long, gold necklace that Izzy picked. I hadn't even considered something like it and it's not designer or anything. It's a necklace she says she bought on holiday once but she can't remember where. Anyway, she held it up to my neck when I was trying on my dress and we agreed it went perfectly.

Izzy, standing next to me, is in a stunning black,

high-neck outfit that I chose for her last minute this morning when she casually mentioned that she still didn't have a dress for tonight, even though I'd told her maybe a MILLION times that she needed one.

"Stop fidgeting," I tell her through gritted teeth, as she pulls the skirt from where it's caught under her shoes. "Smile for the photographers."

She rolls her eyes and does a dopey wave. "How's this?"

"Awful," I say, still grinning like a robot, my eyes watering as I try not to openly laugh at her. "We'll work on it."

The reporters shout at us but we ignore them, heading into Mansion House when we've posed long enough, their questions ringing in our ears: *Is the family falling apart? Are Jackson and Izzy truly welcome at Number 10? Do you hear wedding bells for your parents? How would you feel about becoming stepsisters?*

Gliding up the steps behind the towering columns and through the doors, with Izzy tripping over her feet behind me, I thank the doorman who greets me and take a sparkling water from one of the silver trays.

"Whoa. This place is cool," Izzy says, looking about us. "It's MASSIVE. This is someone's house? Who lives here?"

"This is the official residence of the Lord Mayor of London."

"How come his house is way bigger than yours?"

"What do you mean?"

"How come the Prime Minister doesn't get to live here? Your mum has landed the top job in the country, right? That makes her very important. And this castle/mansion/palace is MUCH better than Downing Street. Not that Downing Street isn't really nice and everything, but this place –" she gestures around, almost knocking someone's glass of champagne out their hand as they squeeze past – "is AWESOME."

I don't want to laugh, because she's being ridiculous, but I can't help it. And you know what? She kind of has a point.

As Izzy rambles on about the columns and the paintings, I watch the other guests milling around, talking to one another and completely ignoring us. A couple of Mum's cabinet members say hello politely as they pass and spot someone more important to talk to, but it strikes me that no one actually bothers to make proper conversation.

Sebastian doesn't even manage a smile when he spots us. It's more of a grimace.

When I think about it, no one has ever really

bothered to talk to me at events like these. I'm just used to standing behind Mum, sipping my drink and trying my best to listen to her conversations. I'm so grateful to have the privilege of going to grand events, I don't really focus on how bored I am at them.

But tonight, I'm not having a boring time, not with Izzy loudly questioning whether I think it would be possible for her to climb the marble columns or do I think they'd be too slippy for her feet to get any grip?

That's when it hits me: *I'm glad Izzy's here.*

What. Is. Happening.

"Oh yes!" She claps her hands excitedly as the procession begins for us to be led into dinner. "Food time! I hope it's good. How many courses do you think it will be? Let's have a bet. I bet ten."

We're shown to our seats in the Egyptian Hall and I'm happy to find that we're opposite each other, and weirdly grateful that we're not on the top table with Mum and the Lord Mayor. It means we're not so on show and there's less risk of us embarrassing her.

The first course arrives – there will be five in total, not ten, much to Izzy's disappointment – and it's a delicious coal-roasted beetroot with pickled dates and grilled asparagus with truffle oil. I eagerly pick up my knife and fork and get stuck in, while chatting to the person on my right about the beautiful flower arrangements on the table.

I notice Izzy examining the contents of her plate as though she's been given a plate of slugs. Pushing the vegetables around with her fork, she stabs at a pickled date and gives it a sniff, before recoiling and dropping her fork so it clatters on her plate.

"*Bleugh*," she mouths to me.

I ignore her, trying my best to focus on talking with my neighbour. It's harder than it sounds with Izzy playing with her food and making a series of dramatic expressions. Eventually I lean forwards to whisper to her.

"You don't have to eat it. Just leave it."

"I can't!" she insists. "I don't want to leave all the food on my plate and show up Patrice. It's rude if I don't eat any of it."

"She won't even know! Stop playing with it and leave it."

Glancing up and down the table to make sure no one else is looking, Izzy checks that her napkin is covering her dress and in one swift movement, uses her fork to sweep the food from her plate into her lap.

"*What are you doing?*" I hiss, stunned at what I've just witnessed.

"Don't worry, this is a great trick," she whispers

smugly, folding up her napkin and pushing back her chair. "I'm going to put this in the bin." She clears her throat and, raising her voice slightly, tells me, "I'm off to use the loo."

"Very good," I say, watching her in dismay.

To my great surprise, her trick works. Everyone around us is too busily engrossed in their own conversations to notice her leave or return, and by the time she comes back, her napkin is empty, the plates have been cleared and she takes her seat happily.

"Mission accomplished."

"Thank goodness no one saw you," I say, keeping my voice down just in case.

"Exactly, I'm super stealthy." She hesitates. "Although one person did see me throwing the food away."

"Who?"

"Sebastian. He came out just as I was about to get rid of it. But he promised not to tell and he gave me the tip to maybe throw it in the bin of the ladies' toilets instead of the one in the hallway. You know, a little more incognito."

"Of COURSE you should be throwing it in the bin in the toilets! Why did you think it was a good idea to just throw it into the first bin you came to?! Anyone could have seen you in the hallway!"

"Yeah, but they didn't. Sebastian was the only one

who saw. Hey, do you think he ever smiles?"

"You're lucky it was only Sebastian," I sigh, spotting the next course on its way out. "Imagine if it had been the Lord Mayor."

"Hopefully the next course will be better. I'm starving!"

But she looks crestfallen at what is placed in front of her, a stuffed aubergine with chickpeas and some fresh coriander garlic. She carves out a tiny bite.

"What's that tangy taste?" she demands, glaring at her plate as though it's betrayed her.

"It's a glaze."

"I can't eat this. Can I ask for pizza?"

"No, Izzy, you cannot ask for pizza. This is *the Lord Mayor's Banquet*."

With a long, drawn-out sigh, she flicks the aubergine into her napkin and is once again up on her feet before I can stop her. A few minutes later she reappears with a dismal expression.

"My stomach is rumbling."

"Don't worry, you'll like the next one," I assure her, attempting to convince myself at the same time.

As the main course is elegantly placed on the tables by the waiters, Izzy makes a face at me.

"Don't they serve normal food? What is this? Gross

gloop?"

"Are you kidding? It looks amazing! Artichoke and couscous *ragout*."

She reluctantly dips her fork into the sauce and licks it as though she's being forced into some kind of torture, before wrinkling her nose and shaking her head vigorously. Checking no one's watching again, she prepares her napkin.

"Izzy, no! Please don't!" I plead desperately.

"Why not? It's working!"

"You have to eat something. And this course is a lot more substantial! You can't carry your entire plate of *ragout* in a napkin! Something will go wrong."

"You see? You're overthinking again. I've already proved to you that this trick works and here you are being all worried and weird."

"I'm being realistic, you can't possibly—"

Before I can finish, she's tipped the contents of her plate into her lap and folded up the corners of her napkin, pushing her chair back hurriedly.

"Need the loo again! Must be all this rich food," she says, a lot more loudly than I would have liked.

As she disappears through the doors, I do a quick check to ensure no one is eyeing her up suspiciously and am pleased to see that she has escaped with her food unnoticed. Sebastian glances up as she leaves, but if he thinks that she may be trying that trick yet again, he doesn't show it. He returns to concentrating fully on the woman to his left, who is gesturing passionately as she talks.

I breathe a sigh of relief and focus on my own food. The *ragout* is spectacular and I'm already excited for the pudding, which, if I remember correctly from the menu, is apple, raspberry and cinnamon tart served with homemade vanilla sauce. YUM. If Izzy doesn't want hers, she can hand it over to me. There's no way I'm going to let that go in the bin.

With neither of my neighbours striking up conversation – they both have their backs turned to me – I hope Izzy comes back soon. She's been longer than she was last time. I finish my food and wait patiently, using the time to admire the amazing décor of the Egyptian Hall.

The plates are cleared, dessert is served and Izzy still hasn't come back. I start to get a little worried, but then I remember that it's Izzy we're talking about here and she's probably got distracted by something or other on her way back to the banquet.

Suddenly, I'm tapped lightly on the shoulder by a waiter.

"Pearl Francis?" he begins, leaning in so I can hear

him over the noise of the hall. "Isabella Williams has requested you join her in the . . . uh . . . bathroom."

I smile at him serenely as I push my chair back. "Thank you."

I calmly make my way round the tables to the doors, pretending as though everything is absolutely fine. But once I'm out the hall and out of sight, I lift the hem of my dress and race towards the bathroom, scenarios playing out in my brain. I KNEW that napkin wouldn't hold. I bet it tore and the food went all over her.

If she has spilled *ragout* down her dress, I will be SO annoyed. Mum's speech is about to start any minute! Lucky for her, I asked Beth to put two spare dresses in the boot of the car, just in case. You see, Izzy? Sometimes it pays to be an overthinker.

I push through the toilet door ready to be proven right, eager to announce to her that I have everything under control and can save the day thanks to my being extra organized. But I am not confronted by the spectacle of Izzy in a *ragout*-stained dress. There is absolutely nothing that I've prepared that can help with this.

The whole of the ladies' toilet is flooded. And the toilet that is spilling over, the one that's caused this total disaster, is clogged with all the food from Izzy's napkin.

CHAPTER FIFTEEN

"WHAT HAVE YOU DONE?" I cry, leaning back against the door to keep it shut.

"It wasn't me!" Izzy yells, her eyes wide with panic.

"Oh, so the toilet happens to be overflowing with someone else's food? This is a Grade One listed building, Izzy! You can't clog up the pipes, they're really old!!"

"Pearl, I SWEAR I didn't put the food down the toilet! I put it in that bin over there!" She points to the bin next to the sink. "I swear I'm telling the truth!"

"How did it end up in the loo then?!"

"I don't know! I came in here and it was like this! Pearl, what do I do?"

"Don't panic," I say, sounding a lot more confident than I am, horrified that the huge pool of water is creeping closer and closer to my shoes as it gushes from the toilet bowl.

"I'm already panicking! I promised I wouldn't ruin tonight for Patrice. I was trying to be on my best behaviour!" Izzy bites her lip. "And now I've broken the building."

"You haven't broken the building," I tell her, desperately trying to think up a solution. "We'll fix it and mop it all up without anyone ever finding out."

Just as I finish my sentence, the door bumps into my back as someone attempts to come in. Izzy and I gasp at the same time. I press back against the door, holding it shut as the person tries again, fiddling with the handle and asking loudly if it's broken.

"I'll handle this," I whisper to Izzy, before clearing my throat and opening the door a fraction to speak through it. "I'm afraid this bathroom is out of order. Please use the one on ... uh ... the second floor. Thank you, bye!"

The woman waiting to come in seems startled at this news and eyes me suspiciously through the crack of the door.

"Is that you, Pearl? The Prime Minister's daughter?"

"No! No, sorry, don't know who you're talking about. I'm a waiter and someone is being really sick in here. You can't come in!"

"Oh my goodness." She puts a hand on her heart. "Is it the food? Should I be worried?"

"No! Not the food! Nothing to worry about! It was

maybe her lunch! Yeah, her lunch food. Not the food here. The food here is delicious. But use another toilet because of the sickness! OK, bye bye, thank you!"

I slam the door shut and turn to see clumps of toilet tissue floating in the water that has by now covered the whole bathroom floor.

"WHY is there toilet tissue everywhere?!"

"I was trying to mop it up while you dealt with her!" Izzy says frantically. "I thought it might help!"

"You thought we could use *toilet tissue* to mop this up?" I bury my face in my hands. "Izzy, look how much water there is! Toilet tissue is not the answer."

"We can google how to fix this," she says, clicking her fingers. "There will be a YouTube video or something, right? There always is. Did you bring your phone? I don't have mine."

"No, it's in my clutch. And by the time we'd watched a video, the room would be destroyed. Try lifting the tank lid to see if there's something in there that stops the toilet flushing."

"GROSS!"

"Don't be ridiculous, Izzy, it's clean water in that top bit!"

Throwing me an untrusting look, she cautiously lifts the lid and looks down.

"Anything that looks wrong yet fixable?" I ask hopefully.

"I don't know how it's supposed to look in the first place," she argues, before getting defensive as I roll my eyes. "You come over and look, if you're so knowledgeable."

"Fine. You guard the door."

We switch places, ruining our shoes in the process as we walk through the water. In the short space of time it takes to cross the bathroom floor, I have to yell twice at Izzy to keep her dress up so the hem doesn't get soaked.

I have no idea how a toilet works or how it should look inside the tank bit, but I want Izzy to think I know what I'm doing, so I pretend to examine it carefully. I put my hand in the water and fish around the components, pretending to check some kind of tube and a random chain.

"Well?" Izzy prompts after turning someone else away from the door.

"Nothing obvious," I say, flicking water off my hand and making my way out of the cubicle to the sinks. "I'll just wash my hands and then I think we're going to have to tell someone. Mum never has to know this happened, we can swear them to secrecy."

I try to turn the tap on, but it's too stiff. I pull harder at it, hurting my hand in the process, then somehow manage to yank it right off.

Water spouts uncontrollably from the sink, soaking us both. I scream, trying to cover the jet of water with my hands, but that somehow makes it worse as it misdirects it, the water spraying all over the mirrors and walls. Izzy tries to help me, putting her hands over mine to make it stop.

Now that the door is unguarded, it swings open and Mum comes in.

"Girls, are you in here? I've been worried about. . ."

Her jaw drops to the floor.

"Patrice, we can explain!" Izzy cries.

But we have both instinctively dropped our hands and the water sprays past us and goes all over Mum, standing in the doorway. She gasps, lifting her arms to shield her face.

Springing into action, I grab some hand towels from the basket next to the sink and run towards Mum, but I slip in the pool of water, sliding across to her, and as I try to regain my balance I reach out my arms to her and together we tumble down on to the floor.

At Mum's cry as we fall, her secret service agents come bursting into the bathroom. Taking in the chaos in front of them, they quickly help us to our feet, pulling us through the door and out into the hallway.

Mum is drenched. Her dress is ruined, much like mine. Izzy follows us out, also soaked. We stand in silence, water dripping on to the carpet, all of us too shocked to speak.

"Oh my god."

Sebastian appears from round the corner with two other senior cabinet ministers, Gabrielle and Jackson. They all stop in their tracks, their eyes scanning from Mum, to me, to Izzy.

"We came to find you, Prime Minister," Sebastian says, baffled. "It's time for your speech."

"Gabrielle," Mum croaks, finding her voice and lifting up her chin, "would you be so kind as to find someone to deal with the plumbing in the ladies' toilet. There are several problems that need to be addressed right away."

"Of course," she says, typing into her phone. "Let me get you another dress. I put a spare in the car as you requested, just in case."

Aha, great minds! I beam up at Mum. She does not smile back.

"Yes," Mum says firmly. "I can't do my speech looking like this."

"I'm so sorry, but I don't think we have time for an outfit change," Sebastian says, checking his watch. "We're on a very tight schedule and your speech was supposed to have already started, hence why we came looking for you."

"I see." Mum purses her lips.

"Perhaps I should do the speech instead?" he suggests.

"Yes, I think that's wise," one of the ministers agrees. "What a shame, Prime Minister! You've written such brilliant words."

"Such a shame," the other minister says. "It really is a wonderful speech and you're such a fantastic speaker."

"I will try my best to do your speech justice," Sebastian says impatiently, checking his watch again. "We had better get back to the banquet. I hope . . . I hope you're all right, Prime Minister."

"I will be, thank you, Sebastian," Mum says, wringing out her sleeve. "And thank you for helping me by stepping up at the last minute. Again."

He smiles graciously and then turns on his heel, racing back towards the hall with the other ministers in tow. Gabrielle makes an excuse to leave, saying that the plumbing will be sorted in no time and hurrying off after Sebastian.

Izzy opens her mouth to speak.

"Please don't," Jackson growls at her.

She duly clamps her mouth shut. Mum inhales deeply before speaking.

"That's the last straw," she says in a calm but firm tone. "I give up. I can't do this any more. It's not working. Jackson and Izzy, I'd like you to move out of Downing Street. Tonight."

Jackson looks shocked. Mum pushes back the damp hair plastered across her forehead.

"Well done, Pearl. Well done, Izzy," she says quietly, her voice faltering. "Looks like you won."

With that, she walks away from us with her agents surrounding her, turning the corner and disappearing from view.

IZZY'S BLOG

We did it.

The plan worked. Patrice and Dad have broken up and we're moving out of Downing Street. Back to our old life.

This is definitely a good thing. We never belonged here and Dad knows it as well as I do. Patrice and Pearl will be so much happier without us. I think Bugsy will miss them and Rosy, but he is going to love his new home. He can go on long walks without being photographed all the time. It will be good for him.

And I definitely will not be missed. The staff here

are probably celebrating. They're probably having a big party. Sure, Tony came to give me a hug just now and he seemed a bit sad, but I think he was doing that for show.

It was quite sweet actually. He said, "You've brought lots of laughter here." Which is a nice thing for someone to say. I always saw myself as quite a sad, broody person, but it looks like here I gave a bit of cheer. So that's good. Anyway, Tony will be pleased he can play serious chess and board games with Pearl again without me getting in the way or asking a million questions. Although I was getting the hang of some of the games. Maybe I can teach Dad.

But it will be great to get back home and look however I want, do whatever I want and be allowed to play my music as loud as I want. I won't be disturbing anyone. Because there won't be anyone to disturb. So that's good.

And I can go back to school. Back to Kylie and Jenna. Maybe they'll be my friends again. It might take time, but I'm sure I can win them over. Although, it has been quite nice having a break from them. I don't know, maybe I spent too long trying to please them rather than being myself. I get this funny feeling in my stomach when I think about seeing them again, like

I'm not all that excited and I'm actually a bit nervous. I'm sure that will change, though, once I'm back home.

I feel bad for Dad. He's really sad about the whole thing. Which I get. But he's got a new series to start filming, so that will keep him busy. We were happy before he got the job here. We can be happy again. It's not a big deal.

I'm just waiting for the car to take us home. I've packed my bags. Technically, they've been packed twice. I packed them and then Pearl came in and made me re-pack them because apparently I did it wrong.

Seriously, she is so weird. We are so different. This is what we wanted. She'll be able to go back to having the house to herself and she can go to events without me ruining them for her. She'll be happy when I'm gone.

She tried to give me the rollerblades back. The ones I got her.

"They're yours," I said, all surprised that she'd try to give them back.

"I can keep them? You don't want them?"

"I've got my own. Anyway, these ones have had your stinky feet in them already. You better keep them."

She laughed at that. "All right then. Thanks."

I thought it was funny how she laughed about it because a few weeks ago she would have been madly insulted if I'd called her feet stinky and would have gone off on one. But now she finds that sort of thing funny. I guess we understand each other a bit better now.

"Thanks for helping me pack," I told her. "I don't really see how the rolling up of all my clothes is any better than my way of squishing them in, but thanks."

"You're welcome. Here, this is for you."

She held out a bag and when I took it and peeked inside there was her chessboard and a new bottle of lavender oil spray.

"In case you have trouble sleeping," she explained.

"Chess is that boring, for sure."

"I was talking about the lavender mist."

"I know." I smiled at her. "Thanks."

She nodded. "Good luck with everything."

"You too."

She seemed all uncomfortable for a moment and I was trying to work out why when she stepped forwards and gave me a hug. It lasted for about a second and was super awkward because she was so tense. I don't think she gives many hugs. Then she left my room and I felt sad for some reason and sat down.

I should be feeling happy. This is what we wanted. It's time for me to go home.

So, how come it feels like I'm leaving it?

CHAPTER SIXTEEN

I've never noticed how loud my footsteps are. How have I not noticed this before? Maybe it's my shoes. When I walk along the corridors of Downing Street, my footsteps are so loud, they echo off the walls. Or maybe it's because it's so quiet now.

"Where is everyone?" I ask Rosy, who is trotting along by my feet.

She sneezes and continues on down the stairs ahead of me. Rosy has spent a lot of time sulking. I think she misses Jackson. And Bugsy. And Izzy. But she still has me. I keep telling her that. She's so beautifully trained now too. She doesn't need Jackson any more. None of us do.

Although ... well, Mum's a bit down, which isn't surprising. Going through a break-up isn't easy (so I hear).

I wanted to talk to Mum after the Lord Mayor's Banquet. I was hoping to explain to her exactly what had happened and how none of it had been on purpose. But she must have left straight after announcing that Jackson and Izzy were moving out, because by the time we got outside her car had gone. Then I couldn't speak to her at home because I guess she was chatting through things with Jackson. The next day, Gabrielle told me Mum was too busy to talk to me.

"She doesn't have five minutes?" I asked hopefully.

Gabrielle gave me a sympathetic look and said gently, "Let her have a bit of time to cool down."

So I left it that day, helped Izzy pack up her things, said goodbye to Jackson and had dinner on my own because Mum was on a call to the President of the United States. I caught Mum at breakfast the following morning and apologized about what had happened at the banquet. She put down her coffee mug and listened while I went through everything in detail.

"I understand. Thank you for explaining it to me," she said.

And then she picked up the newspaper on top of the pile in front of her and started reading while eating a piece of toast.

"That's it? You're not going to yell at me?"

She raised her eyebrows at me. "Do I usually yell at you?"

"Well ... no. But, I thought you might want to this time."

"I don't want to."

"Oh." I didn't know what to do then, glancing around the kitchen aimlessly before blurting out, "I'm sorry about you and Jackson."

"Thank you, Pearl."

"Did you break up? Properly? Or are you just letting things cool—"

"We broke up."

"Oh. I'm sorry."

"Me too." She paused with an expression of sadness, her eyes downcast. "Life doesn't always go the way you want it to."

I went over to her and wrapped my arms round her waist. She held me to her.

"You've still got me," I said, my voice muffled into her side.

"I do. And you're all I need."

It was a nice moment until her phone started buzzing and she had to get to work. Part of me wishes I could tell her all about mine and Izzy's pact to sabotage the household so she can be mad at me, as she should be. I didn't realize I'd feel so guilty seeing her go through losing Jackson. I was so focused on getting Izzy out, I didn't really think about how Mum would go through a break-up too.

I hope Jackson isn't too sad. He's a nice guy. I like him. But they'll realize soon that we did this for them. One day they'll thank us.

I hope.

I can't believe I never noticed how loud my footsteps are! It's all I can hear. Honestly, I stop outside the kitchen and it's like the whole house has fallen silent because I've come to a halt. Was it like this before? It must have been. I've got used to the thump of Izzy's music, or her annoying loud voice, or Bugsy's silly little bark.

I miss that scruffball. Bugsy, not Izzy.

"Hello, Pearl," says Tony, who I find going over some admin in the kitchen. "Here for some biscuits?"

Rosy immediately sits on the word "biscuits".

"I'll have to have one now and give her a bit, otherwise it's cruel," I sigh.

"Sure," he chuckles as I reach for the packet. "You'd better have one for Rosy's sake."

"I was actually wondering what you were up to. Want to play a card game? I learnt a new one from my tutor yesterday."

"Sorry, I'm rushed off my feet. You'll have to wait until

my break this afternoon and, even then, I'm not sure I'll take it today."

"On a Saturday?"

He looks up from his file. "No such thing as weekends in Downing Street. Your mum around?"

"No such thing as weekends in Downing Street," I repeat with a grin, before asking Rosy to do "paw" and giving her a tiny bit of my biscuit as a reward. "Mum's got that big meeting with social workers today."

"Why don't you play with Iz. . ." He trails off. "Sorry, forgot for a moment."

"It's OK, she was awful at everything," I remind him hurriedly. "I'd much rather play with someone else. It's no worries! See you in a bit."

I leave the kitchen with a cheery wave and stand in the middle of the hallway. Rosy comes with me and sits at my feet patiently while I work out what to do. The door custodian gives me a nod of acknowledgement. The grandfather clock nearby ticks irritably.

This is my own fault. I should have been more organized and planned something for the middle of the day. I took Rosy for a long walk this morning, and this evening I'm going with Mum to meet England's women's rugby team. In between, I've got nothing. I don't know how it slipped my mind to plan something.

I guess I'm used to spending this time with Izzy concocting schemes or arguing with her.

"We could read a book or watch a movie," I suggest to Rosy.

Rosy lies down.

"There's no need to look so enthusiastic," I say sarcastically, crouching down to give her an ear scratch. "Come on, Rosy, it's time to stop moping. Don't you love having the house to yourself again? Trust me, this is SO much better."

She sighs.

"I know!" I say loudly, heading to the stairs and calling Rosy to join me. "We can do some rollerblading! That's fun. And I need the practice."

I hear the custodian groan and mutter to himself, but I choose to ignore him. I *may* have accidentally rolled into the hat stand last time, when Izzy was insisting I try going faster, and it *may* have fallen on top of him.

I get my rollerblades, put my helmet and safety pads on, and then cheerily make my way back down to the hall where a minister is on her way to a meeting. When she sees me in my gear, she does a double take.

"How's all that skating coming along?" she asks.

"Don't worry!" I call after her. "I'm going outside so I won't disturb anyone!"

"You never disturbed me!" she calls back, disappearing through a door.

It's very nice of her to say, but the only reason Izzy and I were rollerblading around the house was to cause havoc for our sabotage plan. Now that's been achieved, I'm not going to cause any trouble. No one needs to panic. It's back to just being . . . me.

Once I'm outside with my blades on, I get my balance right and push off, having a little skate around the patio bit where there are paving stones and no grass. I do a few loops and come to a stop, resting my hand on the garden table where Mum has her morning coffee and reads the newspapers in the early sunshine if it's a nice day. I sit down at the table and listen to the birds chirping, while Rosy goes to explore the rose bushes. It's strange. Rollerblading isn't as fun on your own.

I don't know why I feel like something's wrong.

Look, I'm not saying I miss Izzy, because I don't. I have been an only child my whole life and I've loved it. I never felt like I was missing anything. Mum and I work great, just us two. That's the way it's always been. That's how I wanted it.

But maybe I've grown *used* to having Izzy around. That's the difference. I'm not missing Izzy specifically. Things have changed. And change is always confusing.

"Pearl?"

I squint up at Tony as he steps out into the garden and gives me a parcel.

"This just arrived for you, and these –" he holds out his hand to reveal some stolen mints from the Cabinet Room – "are from me."

"Thanks, Tony. You're the best."

"And don't forget it."

He heads back in and I unwrap a mint, popping it in my mouth while I examine the parcel. The handwriting on the front is so messy, it's barely legible. I'm surprised the parcel made it here. I open it excitedly and a large bit of grey material falls out along with a card.

I untangle and shake out the material. I realize it's a onesie. A wolf onesie, to be exact.

I open the card to even messier handwriting that if I squint my eyes I can just about make out.

Hey Pearl,
    I felt bad that you gave me your chessboard and I didn't give you anything. So, here you go. I know how you feel about wolf PJs. Thought you could add this to your collection. I added something to the back of it to remind you of me, haha.
    Izzy

I hold up the wolf onesie and turn it round to look at the back. Pinned to the material is a piece of paper and written across it in bold, black letters is the word "LOSER".

For goodness' sake, she is SO immature.

But it makes me smile anyway.

"This is *brilliant*," I say enthusiastically, standing in the middle of the stage and blinking into the spotlight. "We need more live music venues like this."

"I'm glad you like it," the owner says, beaming at me from the wings while next to him Beth takes a call. "I've put my life and soul into this place. I wanted to protect its history and heritage but breathe new life into it. Some big names played here. Hopefully, more will."

I nod thoughtfully, admiring the space. A long time ago this was a popular venue for up-and-coming singer-songwriters to showcase their music but the building fell into disrepair over the years. The new owner, Eddie, loves all things music and has completely refurbished it. It's due to open next week with a run of sold-out shows. It looks good as new. I can picture the tables full, the lights down, the artists nervously stepping out to where I am now to perform and try to capture their audience.

I was surprised when I was invited to have a private

showing. Technically, Eddie invited Mum and me to come have a look around together, but she couldn't squeeze it in this week and, as the arts are so important to her, she insisted I go without her to represent our support.

I tried as best I could to persuade Mum to come with me. I thought it might cheer her up, doing something a bit more fun than all the meetings she has to sit through. She's been so *down* since Jackson left. I thought she might be sad for a couple of days, but it's lasted for ages. Nothing seems to make her laugh at the moment and I swear she hasn't been sleeping. All she does is work and she has a permanent frown on her face, and she's a lot more short-tempered and snappy these days. Nothing seems good enough.

I don't want to exaggerate, but she's acting more and more like Sebastian every day.

I know. Imagine.

"Honestly, I'm fine. It's a good thing Jackson is gone, Pearl," she told me when I tried to talk to her about the break-up one morning as she rushed about the kitchen making coffee, while reading through an important document. "I've realized I don't have time for a relationship. It's time to focus on the polls."

"Mum, I don't think that's—"

"Gabrielle!" she yelled, interrupting me and rushing out the kitchen. "This initiative is all over the place! We need to sort it now!"

It's as though she's determined *not* to have time for anything or let herself be happy. I'm beginning to think that maybe mine and Izzy's perfect plan wasn't so perfect after all.

Anyway, I hope Eddie doesn't mind that she didn't come to the music venue and that it's just me. I'm not exactly the best person to publicize such a cool place as this. In fact, the best person probably would have been Izzy.

"I know someone who would be really jealous of me being here, standing on this stage," I say, smiling.

"Yeah?" Eddie says. "They like music?"

"She loves it. Very loud music."

He grins. "That's the best way of listening to it."

"That's exactly what she says." I put my hands on my hips. "How do musicians do it? Just standing up here I feel nervous, and I'm not even performing. No one is in the audience."

"It's scary, huh," Eddie says, glancing out at the empty seats. "But I guess once you're out there, playing your music and seeing people enjoy it, it must be a great feeling. I imagine the hardest part is stepping out on to the stage in the first place."

"Yeah. I could never do it."

He looks surprised. "I'd say it's not far off what you do now, isn't it?"

"How do you mean?"

"What you and your mum do is a bit like being up on stage," he explains. "It's being on show, engaging and reading an audience, taking on an important role. Right?"

"Maybe. When you put it like that. I don't always get things right for my audience. Especially recently."

He shrugs like it's no big deal. "Musicians can hit the wrong notes sometimes. It's a journey."

"That's a nice way of looking at it." I smile at him. "You're very wise."

He chuckles. "I'll have to tell my children that you said that. They won't believe me."

"Pearl, it's time to go," Beth says, hanging up the phone and coming over to us. "We have to get to that book launch across town."

"Thanks so much, Eddie," I say, striding back across the stage to shake his hand. "This is a wonderful venue and I have no doubt it will be very successful."

"Thanks for taking the time to see it," he replies, leading us out. "And if you and your friend want to come see one of the shows, just say the word."

I stop as he opens the door for us. "Wh-what did you say?"

"To let me know if you and your friend want to come here one night," he repeats cheerily. "You know, your friend who likes music?"

"Right. Yes. Thank you."

We say goodbye and while we wait for the car to pull up, I have a strange, fuzzy feeling in my stomach. The venue was cool and a show there would be great, but it was Eddie's choice of words that has really struck me. He said I could go there with my friend who likes music.

My friend. Finally.

IZZY'S BLOG

I don't know what to do about Dad.

I've tried everything to cheer him up and nothing's working. I've suggested so many things for us to do, everything that we used to love, but he's like a zombie, moping around and not exactly present. Not really there. I gave him a bit of space at first when we moved back to our old place. There was a lot to do, getting the house back up and running again. It needed a good clean and I had to settle Bugsy in. But then I got busy suggesting all the fun things we could do now that we were free again, and he didn't get excited about any of them.

We went to the smoothie bar, but he barely touched his favourite drink. I've tried movie nights, but they're not the same. He doesn't really concentrate on what's going on in the film, I can tell. He sits there glumly, even through comedies.

It got so bad, I decided I'd try cooking his favourite meal! Yeah, me, COOKING. Pearl would have laughed her head off. Everything went wrong. I got the timings all messed up and forgot to turn on the oven, and I think I even managed to chop the vegetables the wrong way. It was a disaster.

I thought maybe it all going so wrong might have made him laugh a bit, but not even my comedy attempts in the kitchen got a chuckle.

"We'll get a takeaway," he said simply, his eyes glazed over. "I'm too tired anyway."

That's all he is at the moment, too tired. Like all the energy has been drained from him. Sometimes I catch him on his own, his forehead crinkled and his eyes shut tight, as though he's trying hard not to cry. I've heard him crying in his bedroom with the door shut. Hearing that made *me* cry. I hate that he's hurting.

I feel so bad. I thought that this was the best thing for us. I thought by ruining Patrice and Dad's relationship, I was doing the right thing for me and Dad.

Now I'm wondering if ruining it was just the right thing for me.

But there's nothing I can do now. It's over. His heart is broken.

And it's all my fault.

CHAPTER SEVENTEEN

One night, when not even my lavender mist is working and I can't sleep, I plod downstairs to get some water and I hear voices coming from the Cabinet Room.

Mum has late meetings all the time, but she's not here. She's not going to be back until the early hours of the morning because she's at a big charity gala. Everyone else should have left to go home by now.

So who is having a meeting here so late?

I know I should go back to bed, but I'm too curious. Also, I haven't been sleeping that well recently, so all I'll be doing is lying there awake, tossing and turning and bothering Rosy, who was sound asleep when I left her snuggled up in the duvet.

Doing up the zipper on my wolf onesie as it's a bit chilly down here, I tiptoe along the corridor and see that the door of the Cabinet Room is slightly ajar. I carefully position myself so I can't be seen and peer in. My shoulders slump in disappointment when I see it's only grumpy Sebastian and one of the other cabinet ministers, Preeya.

I don't know what I was expecting, but something a little more exciting. They must have had a meeting that's overrun. Maybe they haven't noticed the time.

I'm about to turn and creep back to the stairs when I hear something that makes me stop in my tracks.

"Trust me, Preeya, Patrice is *this* close to resigning. It will be any day now."

The breath catches in my throat. *Mum's resigning?* That can't be right! I carefully move closer to the door to listen in.

"How can you be so sure, Sebastian?" Preeya replies. "Has she said something?"

"Yes. She has."

"What did she say?"

"Oh, she mentioned that she was feeling the pressure and maybe she'd expected too much from herself, that sort of thing," Sebastian says breezily.

"And what did you say?"

"I said very little. I didn't want to agree openly with her, but I did everything in my power to encourage her that she was on the right lines. That she was in over her head."

"Perhaps she was just saying that, though, Sebastian. I'm not sure it means anything."

"Please." Sebastian snorts. "It means everything. At long last, Patrice is doubting herself. I thought the day would never come. And guess who she asked to consider being her successor?"

"I don't have to guess that!"

"Yes, I told her I'd be glad to do my duty for the country and replace her as Prime Minister."

I clamp a hand over my mouth. *I can't believe this! I don't want to believe this!*

"After all," Sebastian continues, "she can't possibly think it's a good idea to stay in the role. She's lost all respect and credibility!"

"I suppose with everything that's happened recently. . ."

"That has simply shown what I knew all along. She was never up to the job. I told everyone that from the beginning. I told you all that we were going in the wrong direction and that she couldn't do it. Did anyone listen to me? No. It was Patrice this, Patrice that. What can she bring to the table that I can't? And all the recent events have proved my point. I should have been given the job from the beginning. I'm a natural leader, am I not?"

"Well, I suppose you've done some speeches."

"I've done a lot more than that," he retorts angrily. "Who do you think guides Patrice in her every move? She leans on me for everything!"

"She welcomes advice, but I hope when you're the Prime Minister you'll do that, too."

"When I'm Prime Minister there will be a lot of changes around here, that's for sure. There will be no children allowed in Downing Street ever again!"

"You mean, for however long you're Prime Minister. The person after you might have children, so I'm not sure you can say 'ever again'."

"Yes, I know, thank you, Preeya," he sighs irritably. "You know what I meant. The point is that teenagers do not belong in 10 Downing Street. She should have banned them from the start."

"I have to agree with you, Sebastian, but there are others who don't feel the same way. That's why I'm surprised Patrice is willing to give up so easily."

"What do you mean?"

"You didn't hear the Chancellor of the Exchequer the other day? She was going on about how much livelier meetings at Downing Street had been and how sorry she was to see that girl – what was her name? Oh yes, Isabella – go. Others agreed that meetings had been a lot more entertaining and enjoyable."

"You must have misheard," Sebastian snaps. "I've heard nothing but complaints about Patrice."

"She's got a lot of sympathy from the public."

"HA! Have you seen the headlines recently?"

"I didn't say the press, Sebastian, I said the *public*. According to recent polls, a lot of people relate to her struggles."

"What struggles? What are you talking about?"

"Life, I suppose. Juggling work, family responsibilities. It's not easy, even for the Prime Minister. All of the recent mishaps have made her seem more approachable, more real. Maybe other people out there are relating to the idea of feeling . . . what did you say she was? In over their heads."

"That's nonsense. Absolute nonsense," insists Sebastian, but he sounds like he's trying to convince himself more than anyone else.

"I'm only pointing out what I've heard. It's good to know all sides of the argument, isn't it?"

"Only when all sides of the argument are credible." He hesitates. "*I'm* approachable."

"Yes, of course. You're very approachable."

"The point is, Patrice has been unreliable. She's had to skip meetings and events—"

"For her family," Preeya interrupts.

"That's hardly an excuse. I expect a Prime Minister to be there. That's what I'll tell everyone."

"I suppose, then, you have my full support."

"I'm glad to hear it. The sooner Patrice resigns, the better. I thought she was going to do it straight after the Lord Mayor's Banquet. She seemed ready to. I suppose she needs to get her thoughts in order and I've been patient this long. I can wait a few days more."

"That was an awful incident," Preeya sighs. "She was drenched! How does that even happen?"

"It happens when food is stuffed down a very old toilet."

"What? Is that what happened? I thought it was a plumbing problem."

"It was. And what a shame."

"Why are you grinning? Sebastian, what did you do?" Preeya asks curiously.

"I gave the plumbing problem a little push. I knew Jackson's daughter was getting rid of the food she didn't like that night by putting it in the bin of the ladies' toilet. Patrice needed some encouraging towards a resignation and I thought one more misadventure from her children might give her a nudge in the right direction. I fished the food out of the bin and put it down a toilet instead. Cue complete disaster!"

OH MY GOD.

It wasn't Izzy's fault after all! It was SEBASTIAN! He ruined that night on purpose!

It takes all my willpower not to storm into the Cabinet Room and shout in his face, but something holds me back. I need to hear more. And if I run in there and confront him now, he'll deny it and pretend I'm making up lies. After everything that I've done recently, who would be on my side? Mum would probably think I was causing more trouble.

I KNEW SEBASTIAN WAS EVIL.

"It was you all along!" Preeya gasps, before bursting into giggles. "I had no idea you had it in you, Sebastian."

"When you're at the top, you have to be ruthless. That's something Patrice will never understand. All that noble ambition gets you nowhere in the end. It was a brilliant plan if I do say so myself. I have to admit, it went better than I could have imagined. She was soaked! And there I was, ready to do the speech. That's the beauty of it all."

"What's your next step? Advise her to resign?"

"And risk turning all her supporters in the party against me? No, I have to tread carefully, Preeya. I need everyone to believe that I am here to save the day. That even Patrice wants me to take the job off her hands. So, I have a little something up my sleeve for tomorrow night."

"The speech she's making?"

"It's on family values, taking place in the auditorium of a prestigious London university. The perfect setting."

"What are you going to do?"

Sebastian laughs. "Now, where would be the fun in telling you that? Let's just say Patrice will face yet another public humiliation."

"She can't survive another one."

"No, she can't. It's just as I planned. Her resignation will be in the bag by dinner." Sebastian lets out a low cackle. "It's time for a new Prime Minister."

CHAPTER EIGHTEEN

"What do you mean she's left?"

I stare in shock at Gabrielle as she gathers up some papers from the desk in Mum's study.

"She left half an hour ago," Gabrielle explains. "She's got a day packed with meetings, events, all sorts. Didn't she tell you? Don't worry, you'll see her at the university event tonight. She's going straight there from her dinner meeting."

"That will be too late!"

"Are you OK?" Gabrielle asks, startled. "Is something wrong?"

"Yes! No! I mean ... I need to talk to Mum. It's important."

"If it's urgent, I can get her on the phone for you. You know that."

I do know that. Mum would step out of any meeting

for me, no matter how important it was. But would she even believe me if I explain all this on the phone? It's so crazy, I'm not sure *I* would believe me.

Sebastian has always been one of Mum's biggest supporters. He's been there at her side through it all, guiding and advising her when she needed it, helping her to navigate the hardest parts of her job and celebrating with her when they hit the mark. And yes, he's always been grumpy, he never smiles and seems to be in a constant bad mood, but that's just *Sebastian*.

Mum's backed him up a million times, defending him when I've been rude about him and insisting that his seriousness is what makes him brilliant. She always says that he thinks the worst about everything and that makes her prepared for anything. But all this time, he was focused on his own ambitions, not thinking about what's best for the country but what's best for him. And he's done it so cleverly that if he wins, Mum will think that it was her doing, not his. She truly believes he's her friend.

Sebastian has betrayed my mum and I HAVE to do something.

I turn on my heel and race upstairs. Mum is never going to believe that Sebastian has betrayed her unless she catches him red-handed. She trusts him and she's a strong believer in giving people the benefit of the doubt. I haven't exactly given her much reason to trust me lately. I have to *show* her what he's up to.

"Come on, Rosy," I say, bursting into my bedroom and finding her curled up on the bed. "We're on a mission!"

She jumps down excitedly, ready for an adventure, and I put her lead on before grabbing my phone and calling Beth.

"Hey! Why are you calling? You know I'm downstairs, right? Just grabbing a coffee and—"

"No time for that, Beth, I need a car please."

"But I don't have anything scheduled for you this morning. You have lessons."

"Not any more. Please, Beth, it's urgent. Can I have a car outside in two minutes please?"

"Of course, but—"

"Thanks!"

I hang up, shoving my phone in my pocket and pulling on my coat, before heading out of my room and running to the stairs, Rosy bounding along beside me.

"Pearl?" My French tutor pops his head out from one of the office doors as I zoom past. "There you are! You're late for—"

"Sorry, Monsieur!" I cry, dodging round ministers on their way to meetings. "I'm sick today!"

The door custodian grins as he swings open the door, wishing me a nice day. A car is ready and waiting as I requested and I jump in with Rosy before the reporters, who spend their day milling around the house, notice.

"Where are we going this morning?" Hal asks cheerily, catching my eye in the rearview mirror as he pulls away.

"Jackson and Isabella Williams' house please," I say firmly.

If I'm going to pull this off, I'm going to need all the help I can get.

Izzy's jaw drops when she opens the door and sees Rosy and me standing there. I probably should have called ahead to let her know I was coming, but my head is in such a muddle I haven't been thinking straight.

Rosy lets out an excited bark and jumps up and down at Izzy, happy to see her again.

"What are you doing here?" Izzy asks, beaming as she gives Rosy a welcoming cuddle and bursts into giggles as Rosy covers her face in slobbery licks. "Come in!"

As I step through the door and unclip Rosy's lead, a blur of grey comes hurtling towards me from nowhere, crashing forcefully into my legs.

"BUGSY!" I bend down to give him a fuss, almost

wanting to cry over how much I've missed him. "Hey there, Mr Bugsy, I've missed you too!"

Once they're done greeting the humans, Bugsy and Rosy immediately launch into an exciting round of zoomies, chasing each other down the hall and then round in circles in the kitchen. We follow them through, laughing at their overzealous playfulness.

"I think they're happy to see one another," Izzy surmises, watching them tumble over each other as they misjudge how fast to take a corner.

"I think you might be right. Is your dad in?"

"No, he's filming, but he'll be back in an hour or so."

There's an awkward pause. I'm trying to work out how to lead into the explanation as to why I'm here without blurting it out. She shoves her hands into the pockets of her oversized faded black denim jacket. I pick a stray dog hair off my grey tailored blazer.

"Your house is really nice," I comment, gesturing around the light, spacious kitchen.

My eyes land on the fridge, which is covered in photos. Izzy offers me a drink and as she gets me a glass of water, I wander over to admire the pictures, scanning all the memories. There are photos of Jackson and Izzy messing about, pulling silly faces at the camera, and some of them on holiday in various places, Izzy waving from the sea or selfies of them at dinner holding colourful drinks with those little umbrellas in.

And then there are older pictures of the family from a few years ago.

"Is that your mum?" I ask, pointing at a picture of a woman hugging Izzy tight from behind, both of them grinning stupidly at the camera.

"Yeah." Izzy nods, handing me my water.

"You look just like her."

"Do you think?"

"Yes. You really do."

Izzy smiles at the picture. "Thanks. So, were you in the neighbourhood?"

"Not exactly." I take a deep breath, turning to her with a serious expression on my face. "I need your help."

"What's happened?"

"It's about Sebastian."

"Grumpy Sebastian?"

"That's the one."

I move over to the kitchen table and take a seat. Izzy sits down opposite me. The dogs finish playing and trot over to us, settling down by our feet.

"I overheard Sebastian talking last night," I continue. "He's bad news, Izzy. It wasn't you who caused the toilet to overflow at the Lord Mayor's Banquet. It was him!"

Her brow furrows in concentration. "What do you mean?"

"He planned the whole thing! He waited until you were back at the dinner and then he fished your food out of the bin and clogged the toilet with it. He wanted us to get in trouble and cause a scene."

"But . . . but that doesn't make any sense? Why would he do that?"

"Because he wants to be the Prime Minister! He's encouraging Mum to resign so he can take over!"

"WHAT?" Izzy stares at me in disbelief. "That's MAD."

"I know! I don't know what to do. I overheard him telling a colleague all of this last night and Mum left early this morning before I could fill her in."

"This is nuts! Sebastian scheming to take over! I KNEW this was going to happen. I should have trusted my incredible instincts."

I raise an eyebrow. "Oh really? You *knew* this was going to happen."

"Yes," she says, nodding stubbornly. "I had a feeling something was off with him. I once saw him peel an apple and then eat the peel on its own before eating the apple! Who does that?! From that point, I knew he was untrustworthy."

"Right, anyway, the worst thing about it is, he's planned something for tonight at a speech Mum is giving. I have no idea what, but he said it was going to embarrass her enough for it to be the last straw after everything we did. She'll resign tonight and he will take over the leadership!"

"Tonight? That's so soon! This is not good," Izzy says gravely.

"No, it's not."

"And you have no idea what his plan is or how to stop it?"

"Not a clue. But I have to do something. That's why I'm here," I admit. "I thought you might be able to help. You see, Izzy... The thing is ... uh ... well ... you know how I like things a certain way?"

"That's an understatement," she says, folding her arms and leaning back in the chair. "You almost bit my head off when I merely *suggested* a different hairstyle for you. And don't get me started on how weird you were about all the paintings in Downing Street being perfectly straight. I saw you correcting them all the time."

"You did?"

"Yeah. I was the one shifting them." She shrugs.

"Wait. You WHAT? That was *you*? I thought I was losing my mind!"

She sniggers. "I know. It was hilarious. Every night before bed, I'd pick a couple of paintings in the house and move the frames ever so slightly so they weren't quite straight. Then I'd see you walk past them, double back, stare at them all confused for ages and then make them straight again."

"I can't believe you. . . Oh, never mind," I huff, trying to push that to the back of my mind. "Look, the point I'm trying to make is, I like things a certain way and I've started realizing that maybe, *maybe*, that way was when you and Jackson were around."

Izzy's forehead crinkles. "Huh?"

"Oh my goodness, can you please CONCENTRATE?! I'm trying to say that I want you two to move back into Downing Street! Honestly, you're so annoying. Why can't you listen?"

"You . . . you want us to move back?" she repeats, her eyes widening in disbelief.

"Yes," I sigh, tapping my fingernails impatiently on the table. She really is dragging this out. "I'm sorry if I was ever rude to you and I'm sorry that I ever wanted you to leave. I don't know what's happened, but somehow the house feels weird now. It's quiet and boring and bland. I think . . . I think I might miss you."

She blinks at me.

"I've never had a friend before," I add quietly.

"Huh," she says eventually, nodding slowly and letting my words sink in. "I'm sorry, too. For judging you and pranking you."

"You did prank me a lot."

"I did. You have to admit the green eyebrows thing was funny. And, to be honest, you pulled it off. Not many people could. But I'm sorry all the same." She pauses thoughtfully. "I don't want you thinking I didn't like your mum or anything at the beginning, that's not why I wanted to leave. I think I felt a bit betrayed by Dad for liking anyone who wasn't *my mum*. If that makes sense?"

"It does."

"Without her, it was me and Dad against the world. Together. That kind of thing. But in the end, being with you and Patrice at Downing Street –" she hesitates – "well, it's the first time I've felt at home since Mum died. I kept telling myself I didn't belong somewhere like that. It turns out, it's the only place I've ever felt like I really belonged at all."

I smile at her.

"Dad has been miserable since we left," she continues. "It's been really bad. He's been moping around, trying to pretend he's all right. It's painful."

"I know, Mum's the same. But I think we have a

shot at making it all better. I think we might be able to come up with a way to make sure Mum keeps her job as Prime Minister AND bring your dad and my mum back together. First things first, we need to think of a clever way to secretly sabotage Sebastian's plan, whatever it is, tonight. So –" I hold out my hand – "are you in?"

She shakes my hand without a moment's hesitation.

"When it comes to sabotage, there's no better team." She grins mischievously. "I'm in."

CHAPTER NINETEEN

I think I'm creeping Mum out. Ever since she arrived at the drinks reception for her speech, I've refused to leave her side, which is a strange experience for both of us.

I can tell she keeps trying to shake me, suggesting I go talk to someone over there who's really interesting or checking if I'm hungry and want to go get something to eat, but it won't work. I am not letting her out of my sight. Not for one moment.

Something's afoot and I need to make sure that Mum doesn't walk right into an embarrassing situation.

("Do you have to keep using the word 'afoot'?" Izzy said earlier when we were working out what to do. "Nobody has used that word for a billion years."

Excuse me, but Sherlock Holmes was not a billion years ago. She is so uncultured.)

It's not like it's that fun for me, being glued to

Mum's side. It means I'm forced to listen to all her conversations, some of which are very long. For example, there are a lot of professors here that she's being introduced to, which is no surprise as the event is being held at a university, but do they need to go into detail with her about business cycle fluctuations now? Can't they save that for ANOTHER time when her teenage daughter isn't standing in on the chat too? Twice now I've had to stifle a yawn while someone chats away, clamping my jaw together so determinedly, my eyes water.

I have a new respect for Maya, who has to stand with Mum at all times and listen to all her conversations. How does she do it?

Mum is currently talking to a guy who looks like the most stereotypical professor you could imagine with his thick-rimmed tortoiseshell glasses and red polka-dot bow tie.

"I quite agree, Prime Minister," he says, pushing his glasses up his nose. "And may I say that we appreciate your support for our pioneering research on the global economic crisis."

"Of course," Mum says.

"This may sound a bit odd, but I'd also like to add in light of tonight's focus that I, personally, appreciate your

245

support for single parents and the family unit. You must be very proud of your mum, Pearl."

He smiles at me, one of the first people to acknowledge my presence.

"Yes, yes I am," I say, caught off guard by being brought into the conversation.

"Do you have children?" Mum asks him.

"Yes, a son. And two stepdaughters. It wasn't easy at first, we had a lot of teething problems when we first combined forces," he chuckles, "but we're getting into our groove now."

"You ... you had trouble bringing the two families together?" Mum asks, trying her best not to sound overly eager for the answer.

"Of course!" he replies, looking confused that she might imagine otherwise. "Change is never easy for anyone, and the number of things you're trying to juggle, my goodness it can go wrong! I remember once I came home to find a load of frogs in the house; they were everywhere. The work of my son, I believe, trying to upset the two girls. Didn't work, of course. They enjoyed having all these frogs hopping about the place, wherever you looked. It *was* very stressful collecting them back up." He pauses, choosing his next words carefully as Mum waits, enraptured. "I don't want to overstep the mark, Prime Minister, but if you want my opinion – and I appreciate it's not a very important one – I think you're doing a very fine job. With the country and as a parent."

I nudge Mum with my elbow. "I think that, too."

"Thank you," Mum says, her eyes gleaming at him.

If she is thinking of resigning, like Sebastian is so sure of, then comments like that from the professor must mean a lot to her. It's as though he's reminding her that she's only human and he, like others, recognizes that. Maybe I should tell her how great a mum she is more often.

"Ah, there you are, Prime Minister!"

I freeze at the sound of Sebastian's voice behind us. I hadn't seen him yet tonight and part of me had hoped he had changed his mind. I slowly turn to look up at him. I wish I could tell him what I know, but we need to catch him red-handed.

"Sebastian," Mum says, before gesturing to the nice professor, "have you met—"

"Everyone in here thinks they're the experts," Sebastian says pompously, cutting her off and dismissing the professor with a wave of his hand. "I've had at least two people come right up to me to talk about national policy, as though they know better than us. Honestly,

I'm not sure *mingling* is ever a good idea when you're in our position."

Maya and I share a look while the professor politely smiles and steps away to join another cluster of people nearby. Sebastian pulls at his shirt collar, which looks a little tight this evening, and straightens his mustard-yellow tie.

"Hello, Sebastian," I say through gritted teeth, just to remind him that I'm here at Mum's side.

"What? Yes, hello," he replies impatiently with an irritated glance at me. "I didn't realize children were allowed at this event."

"Sebastian, why don't you try enjoying yourself?" Mum suggests with a knowing smile. "I've had the most wonderful conversations this evening."

"Whatever you say, Prime Minister," he grumbles, before coughing into his handkerchief. "I like to think that I can handle things without the help of a bunch of people who don't know any of the facts and think they're superior because of a few bits of research. I know what I'm doing, thank you very much."

"You mean 'we,'" I correct calmly.

"I'll be happy when this evening is over," he continues, ignoring me. "Then everything will be ... better." He gives Mum a tight-lipped smile. "I had better go and check that it's all set up and ready to go."

"Thank you."

He leaves us to it, weaving his way through the crowd, stopping at the back of the room to talk to Preeya. I swallow the lump in my throat. Suddenly, Mum inhales sharply.

"What is it?" I ask, spinning to face her and grabbing her arm. "What's wrong?"

"Nothing," she says, craning her neck to peer over everyone. "I thought I saw ... I could have sworn I saw Izzy! Over there, near Sebastian!"

"Mum, don't be ridiculous."

"I'm not being ridiculous, it looked just like her!"

"You need your eyes tested," I say, laughing it off. "Why would Izzy be here? Oh, look, there's Gabrielle!"

Mum shoots me a suspicious look, but quickly collects herself as Gabrielle appears in front of us with someone she wants Mum to meet. While they become embroiled in conversation, I glance back across the room to where Sebastian is still talking to Preeya and see Izzy dressed as one of the waiters standing right behind him with a tray of canapés, carefully following his every move without him noticing. She catches my eye and winks, before turning her attention back to Sebastian.

It was Izzy's idea to get in using the catering staff. I had to pull some strings, but luckily the manager of the catering company is a big fan of both my mum and fascinating mysteries. I explained to him that something was AFOOT ("Now you're just saying it to annoy me," Izzy muttered) and we didn't want him to be involved but if he wouldn't mind letting Izzy join his waiting staff for the evening we'd be much obliged. He agreed straight away.

"I think it's fantastic," he said eagerly. "Full of intrigue! If you write a book about this someday – how you foiled an evil plot to overthrow the Prime Minister – will you mention me?"

Izzy's only instruction was to follow Sebastian at all costs and not to let him out of her sight. She had to watch him like a hawk. If he did anything suspicious, she had to call me straight away. Likewise, if anything seemed unusual around Mum, I had to phone Izzy.

"I mean it, Izzy, you have to make sure you stay on it and don't get distracted like usual," I said sternly in her kitchen earlier.

"What do you mean? I don't get distracted."

"It has taken us about an hour to get this far and all we've decided on is I'll watch Mum and you'll watch Sebastian. And it's because you keep changing the subject or going off on a tangent."

"That's not true! I am very focused," she said

defensively, before her eyes drifted to Bugsy curled up on the floor. "Look how his nose twitches in his sleep!"

I didn't have high hopes.

So far, however, she's done well to keep close to Sebastian without him noticing she's there. He might recognize her if he bothered to be interested in anyone but himself, but thankfully he's stayed true to his character this evening.

"Right, we should head backstage and get ready for the speech," Gabrielle says, checking her watch. "They're going to call everyone through to the auditorium to take their seats in a moment."

"I'll come with you!" I say, maybe a tad too enthusiastically.

Mum gives me a strange look. "If you want."

I follow her through the doors to the backstage area, staying so close to her that I accidentally stand on the back of her heel, causing her to wince in pain. While she's having her microphone sorted, I hear a voice come through the speakers of the reception hall telling everyone to take their seats as the speech will commence in five minutes.

I rub the back of my neck nervously, my eyes darting around the back of the stage, trying to spot anything strange or unusual. If Sebastian wants to humiliate Mum publicly, it has to be something to do with her being on stage. I considered whether he might have hired people to run on and throw a bucket of custard at her or something, but her security is so tight there's no way anyone would be able to get through.

"What about a whoopee cushion?" Izzy said earlier, clicking her fingers.

"What about it?"

"That could be it."

"That could be *what?*"

"The thing that Sebastian has up his sleeve!" She looked at me as though she'd cracked the case wide open. "Your mum goes out on stage, she sits down on a whoopee cushion, it makes a big fart noise and next thing you know, she's resigning."

"A whoopee cushion? That's the big, genius plan you think the First Secretary of State has come up with?"

"It could be," she said, stroking her chin thoughtfully. "It's about as believable as your bucket of custard theory."

We disagreed and then, thankfully, moved on with the conversation.

"Hey, Mum," I say, sidling up to her as the sound guy clips her microphone to her jacket lapel, "you don't have to sit on the stage at all, do you?"

"No," she replies, confused. "I'll be standing at a lectern doing the speech."

"So, just to confirm, there's no chance of you sitting on anything?"

I am clearly desperate to be even considering the whoopee cushion theory. But we can hear the audience filling their seats and chatting away out there with the speech imminent, and so far I haven't got a clue what Sebastian's plan is.

"Are you all right, Pearl?" Mum asks, putting her hands on her hips. "You're acting a bit strangely this evening. A bit jumpy."

"I'm fine. Thanks." I bite my lip as the crowd begins to settle into a quiet murmur and someone nearby prepares to go on to make Mum's introduction. "How are you feeling about the speech?"

"Good. Ready. It's almost time to go on."

"You're going to be brilliant," I assure her, not feeling so confident. "And above all else, Mum, I want you to know that you're the best Prime Minister and I don't think that you should forget that or give up."

She blinks at me.

"Not that you ever give up," I add hurriedly, not wanting her to know I'm aware of any resignation thoughts. "But just in case I had caused you to doubt any of that recently. I want you to know that you are exactly what we all need."

She's so taken aback, she's speechless.

"Are you all set?" Gabrielle asks her, appearing at her side. "One of the university professors is going to introduce you any minute."

"Yes, ready, thank you, Gabrielle."

I glance at Mum's empty hands. "Where's your speech? Is it on the lectern?"

"No, it will be on the teleprompter. That's what Sebastian went off to prepare."

"*What?*"

"Sebastian is arranging for the speech to come up on the teleprompter."

"So . . . you didn't memorize it? And you don't have any notes?" I squeak.

"The magic of technology, eh?" Mum says, chuckling at me along with Gabrielle. "I know how you love to make notes, Pearl, but don't worry, I'm in safe hands."

Oh no. That's it! That has to be it! Sebastian is going to do something, delete the speech entirely or change the words so Mum reads out the wrong thing! She's going to be out there on stage on her own and she's going to completely humiliate herself!

The audience begins clapping as the professor introducing Mum steps out on to the stage and heads over to the lectern to welcome everyone.

I scramble to get my phone out of my pocket and call Izzy right away but she doesn't pick up. It reaches voicemail, so I hang up and then try calling her again, but she doesn't answer this time either.

I KNEW THIS WOULD HAPPEN. I TOLD HER SHE'D GET DISTRACTED.

"Izzy! You are *so annoying!"* I snap angrily at my phone as I rapidly send her a text about Sebastian and the teleprompter.

"What did you just say?" Mum whispers behind me. "Did you say something about Izzy?"

I turn to face her. "Mum, you can't go out there. You can't go out on stage."

"Pearl, what is going on?"

Suddenly, there's a loud clanging noise from up in the control booth behind the audience seats. The lights on the stage switch to disco lights and loud pop music begins blaring out of the speakers. The woman doing Mum's introduction clamps her hands over her ears and members of the audience begin laughing. Maya speaks to one of her security colleagues through her headset, trying to work out what's going on.

Mum looks at me accusingly. "I knew I saw Izzy earlier. You two are up to your old tricks!"

Leaving Gabrielle standing there baffled, Mum storms out of the wings and back into the corridor, hurrying to get upstairs to the lighting and sound booth, while Maya and I follow hot on her heels.

"Mum, wait!" I call out. "You have to understand! It's not what you think!"

She marches on determinedly and furiously swings open the door to the control booth with me tripping over my feet to pile in after her. We both gasp at the sight that greets us.

Izzy is standing over the switches of the control booth pressing buttons while Sebastian lies next to her on the floor, groaning in pain.

"Hi, Patrice!" Izzy gives Mum a cheery wave. "Miss me?"

CHAPTER TWENTY

"What on EARTH is going on?" Mum cries, her eyes darting wildly between the pair of them. "Sebastian!"

I stop her from rushing forward to help him up as he groans again, rubbing the back of his head and pushing himself up on to his knees. The silver tray that Izzy was carrying earlier is on the ground next to him, canapés scattered everywhere.

"Are you all right, Sebastian? What happened?" Mum asks, while Sebastian gets to his feet.

"Hang on a second," Izzy says, pressing more buttons. "I'll explain everything in one moment."

The lights go from colourful disco beams to pitch black, to bright white, to spotlights all over the auditorium, and back to disco lights again. Meanwhile the pop music switches to opera and then rock and then R&B until eventually Izzy goes, "AHA!" and presses two buttons. The music stops and the lights return to normal.

On stage, the professor looks relieved and announces to the audience that she'll be with them in a moment before she races off into the wings where, no doubt, Gabrielle is busy panicking.

"There you go," Izzy says proudly, turning to face us properly. "Sorry. Sebastian fell on the switches when I hit him on the back of the head with the tray."

"You WHAT?" says Mum.

"Lightly. It was more of a bop than a hit," Izzy assures her, while Maya stands behind us looking absolutely delighted at Sebastian's plight. "He was being overdramatic."

"*How dare you?*" Sebastian seethes, leaning back against the wall, his hair sticking up all over the place, his face as red as a tomato. "HOW DARE YOU?"

"How dare *you?*" Izzy retorts, crossing her arms.

"Izzy! What is going on?" Mum demands to know.

"What is going on is that your girls are completely UNRULY!" Sebastian explodes. "They are OUT OF CONTROL! For weeks they have been causing CHAOS in Downing Street where chaos does not belong! Children and politics DO NOT MIX!" He points his finger at Mum. "How could you let this happen? How could you possibly think you were fit for the job when you can't even CONTROL THESE CHILDREN?"

"Sebastian, I—"

"I WON'T STAND FOR IT ANY LONGER!" he bellows, flailing his arms around. "No one will! Patrice, you are no longer wanted as Prime Minister! Not by the country, not by the government, not by ME! YOU MUST RESIGN TONIGHT!"

The room falls into stunned silence as his outburst concludes.

"There's really no need to shout, Sebastian," Izzy says haughtily. "And if anyone should be shouting, it should be Patrice."

"I don't understand," Mum says, rubbing her forehead. "Izzy, why would you hit Sebastian round the head with a canapé tray?"

"Because I followed him in here and I thought something was a bit fishy when he ordered all the sound and lighting technicians to leave," Izzy explains. "They were all like, 'But why?', and Sebastian did his standard grumpy yelling thing until they left. Once they'd gone, I sneakily pushed open the door to see what he was up to and saw him looking around for the teleprompter controls. And, no surprises here, he went to switch it off. That's when I hit him over the head with the tray (lightly). He fell on to the controls, made everything go crazy and here we are."

"But … none of this makes sense," Mum says, frowning at Sebastian who is staring at the floor, his lips pursed.

"Actually that all makes perfect sense," I tell Mum, Izzy nodding along encouragingly. "Mum, Sebastian isn't your friend. He wants you to resign so that HE can become Prime Minister."

"That's why he clogged up the toilets at the Lord Mayor's Banquet. He wanted to cause another scene and embarrass you. He made it look like it was our fault and all along it was him," Izzy says.

"Sebastian?" Mum looks at him in disbelief. "Is this true?"

"He wanted to ruin tonight for you, too," I say when he refuses to speak. "I overheard him telling Preeya his plan last night in the Cabinet Room. You were going to step out there tonight with no notes and no speech, thinking the words would be up on the screen for you, but he was going to make sure nothing was there. You'd be stuck on the stage with nothing to say."

"He knew you were already thinking that maybe the best thing to do would be to step back and if something disastrous happened tonight, maybe that would have been the nudge you needed," Izzy sighs, glaring at Sebastian.

"And then he would have supported your decision before becoming Prime Minister himself," I say angrily. "Mum, he's been pretending to be your friend the whole time, but he was out for himself."

"Sebastian," Mum says, her expression darkening, "do you have anything to say to all this?"

"It's lies," he mumbles unconvincingly. "It's a pack of lies. Children always lie. You know that. They've never liked me. They're pinning all of this nonsense on me."

"Mum," I say, looking directly into her eyes, "Izzy and I are telling the truth. I promise."

"We wouldn't lie to you, Patrice," Izzy says. "To prove it, I'll own up to the fact that it was me who borrowed that big dish thing from the Cabinet Room. That's the truth and so is this stuff about Sebastian."

"Wait, *what?*" I yell, rounding on her. "The dish thief? That was YOU?"

"I didn't realize it was such a big deal."

"It is a PRICELESS DISH that was presented as a GIFT a very long time ago! Mum's got police detectives on the case!"

"Oh, well, you can tell them that it's in my old room in the bottom drawer," Izzy says casually. "I was keeping it there until I worked out what to do with it. Forgot to take it out when I left."

"WHY did you take it in the first place?!"

"I thought it looked nice."

"Are you OUT OF YOUR MIND? You can't just steal stuff from the Cabinet Room!"

"I didn't steal," she corrects, waggling her finger at me. "I *borrowed*. I was going to put it back if it didn't go with my stuff. It never left the house. Why are you obsessed with this dish, Pearl? It's just a round thing, you don't need to be so shouty."

"You are so—"

"All right, girls, all right, that's enough!" Mum interrupts, holding up her hands. "There's a lot of information to process and we should stay on topic."

"You see?" Sebastian spits, pointing at us. "This is ABSURD!"

"Sebastian," Mum begins, clasping her hands together, "I'm afraid you're fired."

He recoils. "*What did you say?*"

"You're fired. Effective immediately. You've been plotting against me and I can't have someone advising me who I don't trust. You've attempted to sabotage two very public events, including almost destroying the plumbing in a Grade One listed building and potentially causing a huge amount of damage to the Lord Mayor's residence on purpose."

"Oh, come ON!" He throws his hands up in the air. "You're honestly going to believe the word of these two . . . these two . . . TEENAGERS over me? Teenagers lie all the time!"

"The only liar in this room is you, Sebastian. You've lied to everyone and I'm extremely disappointed in you."

"Oooooh bad luck, Sebastian," Izzy grimaces. "Disappointment is so much worse than anger."

"So true," I agree.

"These two girls ruined everything! Don't you remember all those meetings they disrupted? All those events they destroyed?" he shouts at the top of his lungs. "They started it!"

"Now who sounds like the child," I point out.

"I don't remember them ruining much," Mum says, to my surprise. "If you're talking about the dinner with the royal family, I distinctly remember the Queen saying she hadn't had so much fun in a very long time. Or perhaps you mean the rollerblading? I recently spoke to the Chancellor of the Exchequer who has since purchased a pair for herself, inspired by these two. Taking a moment away from work to rollerblade down her street apparently helps to clear her mind and encourage motivation."

"Oh please, this is drivel!" Sebastian claims, looking uneasy. "No one is happy about the situation! That smelly, disgusting rescue dog running around—"

"Bugsy is a member of the family," Mum snaps, narrowing her eyes at him. "So please refrain from insulting him. And I'll have you know that studies have proven that dogs can lift the spirits and reduce both stress and anxiety. Very helpful in such a high-pressured environment I'd say, especially according to several of the ministers. Since Bugsy left, Rosy has been inundated with cuddles from MPs who need a moment of comfort. When we had two in the house, it was much easier."

"So what you're saying," Izzy begins cautiously, "is that Pearl and I maybe helped things?"

"Yes, Izzy, that's exactly what I'm saying," Mum confirms. "I don't think much of your methods and there are some things I think we could do differently, but the truth of the matter is that you two brought some light relief, plenty of laughter and a bit of family normality to 10 Downing Street. Almost everyone I've spoken to recently has said so."

"ENOUGH OF THIS SENTIMENTAL, SLUSHY NONSENSE!" Sebastian cries out. "Prime Minister, are you resigning or not?!"

She looks him dead in the eye. "I am not. And I seem to remember firing you."

His eyes widen to saucers, his cheeks puff out indignantly and he looks as though he might implode at any second.

"Maya," Mum says calmly, as Maya stands to attention, "would you mind asking someone to escort Mr Webber off the premises?"

"With absolute pleasure, Ma'am." Maya grins, stepping aside to speak into her headset.

"Sorry, Sebastian," Izzy says, giving him several sympathetic pats on the back. "Your plan was foiled."

"*Gerroff me!*" he snaps, batting her away. He straightens his tie and narrows his eyes at Mum. "You are making a giant mistake. This is it, then? You're really taking the word of two children over me?"

"Yes, Sebastian," Mum says coolly. "I am."

"You'll regret this, Patrice!"

Two security guards arrive and Mum and I step back to let them through.

"DON'T TOUCH ME!" Sebastian yells at them before they do anything. "I'm perfectly capable of walking out myself! If you lay a finger on me, I shall sue! I shall sue you all!"

His jaw set, he stomps past us and marches away,

flanked by the security agents who completely ignore his shouting and bellowing.

As we watch him go, Mum gasps and I burst out laughing. Stuck on the back of his suit jacket is a sign reading, "THE BIGGEST LOSER EVER".

"What can I say?" Izzy smiles. "I couldn't resist."

CHAPTER TWENTY-ONE

"Prime Minister, there you are!" Gabrielle catches her breath, appearing in the doorway of the control room. "I've been looking everywhere for you. Are you ready for your speech?"

"Yes, of course she is," I say proudly as Mum collects herself. "Izzy, you can get it up on the teleprompter, right? If not, we can track down one of the tech people. I'm sure they're lurking around here somewhere, even if Sebastian sent them away."

"Sebastian sent the tech people away?" Gabrielle looks confused. "Why would he do that?"

"Because he's a stupid . . . stupid-head!" I reply.

"Good one, Pearl," Izzy says, rolling her eyes, before leaning over the controls once again. "Yeah, I'm sure I can work out how to sort the teleprompter. Just give me a few minutes."

"Actually," Mum says, clearing her throat and straightening her jacket, "that won't be necessary. I don't need the teleprompter."

"But you don't have any notes."

"I know. I'm going to wing it."

Izzy seems impressed. Gabrielle looks as horrified as I feel.

"*Wing it?*" she repeats, making sure she heard Mum correctly. "You're going to wing the speech? But . . . why?"

"Because that speech was written with someone who has proven himself to be a weasel, and I don't need to say the words of a weasel. I'll say my own words. Pearl and Izzy, we'll chat about all this after the speech, but for now –" she pauses, a smile spreading across her face – "*thank you.*"

With that she quickly turns and leaves the room, heading back towards the stage with Maya and Gabrielle, Gabrielle firing a million questions at her about Sebastian as they walk.

"Wow," Izzy says, exhaling and shaking her head in disbelief. "I can't believe we did it. We actually did it."

"I know. Well done for stopping Sebastian before he got to the controls. Imagine, if he'd had his way, Mum would be on stage right now, floundering without a script and soon about to resign, believing it to all be her fault."

"I don't know," Izzy says thoughtfully. "I think she would have been OK. I think his plan kind of sucked in the end. I was expecting something a little more epic. Turning off the teleprompter? It's hardly a genius plot to ruin someone. Patrice is good on her toes. She would have thought of something on the spot."

"Now that I think about it, I have to agree. Maybe if he'd had one of us on his team, he could have been a bit more creative when it came to the sabotage. Like, someone could have skateboarded on to the stage and knocked Mum off her feet during the speech."

"Good one! Or a classic whoopee cushion, perhaps."

"What is it with you and whoopee cushions?"

"I think they're hilarious. In fact, I plan on buying one very soon and using it on you when you least suspect it."

"Please don't do that."

"You'd be mortified."

"Izzy, I mean it, please don't do it."

"Your worst nightmare. I can picture your face now."

"*Izzy.*"

"All right, calm down, I'll prank Tony with the whoopee cushion instead," she says, before glancing down nervously. "If I see Tony soon, that is."

I nudge her with my elbow. "You will. I'll make sure of it."

She smiles. "Come on then, let's pull up a chair and get ready for your mum's big speech. We've got a great view of the stage here. I can't believe she's winging it after all that."

"It makes no sense," I admit, hopping up on a chair next to Izzy and looking through the glass window at the stage where Mum is stepping out to great applause. "Why would she risk it?"

"It's like she said, she wants to do this herself," Izzy explains with a shrug.

"Good evening," Mum begins, placing her hands either side of the lectern as the crowd falls into silence. "I'm sorry about the delay there. Like so many things recently, this evening hasn't quite gone to plan –" cue laughter from the audience – "but I've found that life rarely does."

She pauses, taking a deep breath, relaxing her shoulders and looking up at the sea of faces watching her. She notes the cameras pointed at her either side of the stage, the red lights blinking as they record. She smiles and steps around the lectern so she can stand in front of it, closer to her audience, nothing between them and her.

"I had written a speech for tonight about family, which is the official reason I'm here," she continues boldly. "My advisers and I sat down for several hours to put together the perfect words on the importance of family and the values we think need to be discussed. It was truly a thoughtful, concise, well-planned speech. But, as I've just mentioned, life doesn't often go to plan. Neither does family. So, I've decided to talk to you tonight without a speech. Without any plan. I'm winging it."

There's a ripple of murmurs through the crowd.

"You see, that speech we'd written was great in some ways, but it wasn't as honest as I'd like it to be. I want to be honest with you tonight. So here goes –" she glances up at the control booth and smiles to herself, as though she can't quite believe what she's about to do – "I have had a really rough few weeks with my family. I've been really struggling."

There are some gasps from those stunned by her honesty, but as I crane my neck to try to see how people are responding, I mostly find everyone enraptured, leaning forward in their seats, eager to hear more.

"You see, I thought that introducing a new partner and his child into my life at Downing Street with my daughter would be hard. But it wasn't just hard. It was near impossible. It was completely disastrous –" there are titters of laughter and nods of solidarity – "I couldn't get anything right. I was trying so hard to be the perfect leader in so many ways. I wanted to be in control, to be the person that everyone looked to for guidance, to make the right decisions – and I'm not talking about being Prime Minister here, I'm talking about being a mother!"

She waits for the laughter and clapping to die down before continuing.

"I thought I could control what was going to happen in my home. I thought I was the best person to iron out any problem, to come up with the right solution. But it all got out of control. Everything was a big mess. There were days that I had no idea what I was doing. I felt a bit lost. Like I was getting it all wrong. It turned out, I couldn't plan how to bring these two families together in the perfect way. Just like tonight, I couldn't foresee how so much would go wrong in the lead-up to making what appeared to be a straightforward speech. But, as luck would have it, the way things have gone this evening has shown me what was staring me in the face all along."

She pauses, her audience waiting in silent anticipation.

"The past few weeks have reminded me that change is terrifying and bumpy, but can also be fun and uplifting. I've been reminded of the importance of trust, love, occasional silliness and being human; that it's OK to make mistakes, and, trust me, I have made a LOT of mistakes. Everyone does. Even the Prime Minister. Even mums." She pauses for more laughter from the audience. "When it comes to family, there is no script, no plan, no perfect way of doing things. It's all about winging it. That's what I've learnt over the last few weeks from two brilliant, often exasperating, but totally extraordinary girls."

Next to me, Izzy sniffs.

"So, the most important thing I want to say to you about family," Mum says gently, "is that mine has taught me I don't have to go it alone. That's what family is about. Families are all different, most are dysfunctional, but the point is that you're there, together. There are no rules for what makes a family. But I can tell you this." Her eyes twinkle in the spotlight as she looks up at the control booth. "You know when you're in one."

As the auditorium erupts with applause, I stealthily wipe a tear from the corner of my eye and then join in the clapping. Izzy is up on her feet cheering and whooping so loudly, she's going to burst my eardrums. I push myself up from my chair to join her but before I get the chance to put my hands together, Izzy has leapt on me, giving me a gigantic hug that nearly knocks me backwards, all the while screaming in my ear, "SHE DID IT! SHE DID IT! AND SHE WAS AMAZING!!"

When Izzy pulls away and starts dancing around the booth, I get the chance to have a look at everyone's reaction. I've never seen an audience respond to one of Mum's speeches like this. Everyone is going CRAZY. Mum gives a small embarrassed bow of her head as she receives a standing ovation, before waving and attempting to thank her audience over the noise, but she's drowned out by their appreciation. It takes her ages to walk off the stage because there's no sign of the applause dying down.

"Come on!" Izzy cries, grabbing my arm and yanking me out of the room. "Let's go find her!"

We run towards the stage, but Mum is already on her way to find us and soon the three of us are engulfed in one big hug.

"You were brilliant!" Izzy exclaims, and I can tell that Mum is shocked at such a warm reaction from her, but over the moon to receive it.

"You really were, Mum," I say. "You were the best ever!"

"It's all down to you two." She laughs, pulling back and beaming down at us. "You were my inspiration. I can't believe what's just happened. I'm still trying to get my head around everything. What a night!"

"And it's not over yet," Izzy says with a mischievous grin.

"That's right. Mum, we have one more surprise for you."

"Uh-oh." She narrows her eyes at us. "You haven't adopted another dog, have you? I'm not sure poor Tony could take all that hoovering."

"No, that's not it. But you do have to come with us now."

She frowns in confusion. "But—"

"Don't worry," I interrupt. "I already cleared it with Gabrielle earlier today. Your schedule is ours for the night. Everything else can wait for tomorrow."

"That's right, Patrice," Izzy says as she takes one of Mum's hands and I take the other, dragging her towards the door where her car is waiting. "Tonight is all about family. What could go wrong?"

IZZY'S BLOG

THEY GOT ENGAGED!!!!

My dad and Patrice are engaged!! And it was the BEST PROPOSAL EVER, even if I do say so myself because HELLO the whole thing was MY IDEA.

OK, fine, it was Pearl's idea, too.

PEARL, STOP READING THIS OVER MY SHOULDER. Yes, you are!!! OK, if you aren't reading this over my shoulder, how did you know that I'd written about the proposal being my idea?! I do NOT talk out loud as I write. Go back to reading your old, boring book.

ANYWAY...

What was I saying? Oh yeah, the proposal. It was amazing. We had the whole thing planned out. When Pearl was at my house asking for help with everything to do with Sebastian, we also hatched a cunning plan to get Dad and Patrice back together, and we needed Dad to be in on it. So once he got back from filming, I sat him down, explained everything and guess what? He didn't even hesitate. Of course he wanted to propose to Patrice! That's why he had the ring I found. Obviously, Pearl and I ruined those original plans, but whatever, the point is, he was game as long as Pearl and I were happy with it and DUH now we were.

So, after Patrice's big speech, which was AWESOME and is already a huge trend on social media with everyone being like, "She's the best Prime Minister ever!", we got her in the car and drove to her and Dad's old school. I know, right?

Adorable.

Then she got out the car and she was super confused, looking around her and going, "Why have you brought me here? Am I doing another speech I don't know about?" and we didn't say anything, we just led her into the school hall which was pitch black. Then we switched the lights on and...

There was Dad, right in the middle of the hall, with Rosy and Bugsy!

The whole place was lit up with beautiful candles and fairy lights. Dad had gone all out, it looked AMAZING. I think it's very impressive that he did all that, especially the candle part, because a couple of years ago he actually set his sleeve on fire that time he thought it would be nice to have some candles lit around the house and...

HEY! What do you mean, like father like daughter? EXCUSE ME, PEARL, but I seem to remember that we were BOTH responsible for the tiny fire in the Downing Street kitchen. We've been over this a hundred times!!

STOP READING OVER MY SHOULDER. This is PRIVATE.

Pearl is a stinkhead.

Hahahahaha that got her to look away all

277

grumpily. As I was saying, there were beautiful lights everywhere and it was all romantic and gross and stuff, and Patrice was SHOCKED. Her mouth was wide open and she was looking around her, baffled. Rosy and Bugsy were straining at their leads to get to us, so Dad let them go and they came bounding across the floor and Patrice sort of wandered forwards to where Dad was still waiting for her in the middle of the hall.

He said, "Patrice, this is where we first met, so I thought it would be an appropriate setting for what's about to happen. I can confirm that I have permission from Pearl, Izzy, Bugsy and Rosy, so there's only one thing left to do."

Then he got down on one knee, got out the ring from his pocket and proposed!! And Patrice said YES!!!

It was the best moment ever. They hugged and then Pearl and I ran over to join in on the hug and then Bugsy and Rosy didn't want to be left out so they came scampering over and jumped up at our legs, and everyone was very happy. Patrice was beaming at us, the biggest smile on her face ever, asking how on earth this all came together. Dad said it was all our idea...

That's when Pearl decided to apologize for trying

to ruin their relationsh—

FINE. There's no need to be so shouty, Pearl.

That's when Pearl and I BOTH decided to apologize for ruining their relationship. We explained how we thought it was a bad idea at first and so we purposefully went about sabotaging everything so Patrice would force me and Dad to leave.

In the end, I said, we realized that we'd got it wrong. We were family now.

I looked at Patrice when I said that last bit.

She and Dad then got all teary-eyed and they both went on about how this was better than they could have ever dreamed, blah blah blah.

Dad took me aside then and kissed my head and said he was really proud of me. He said that Mum would be proud of me, too.

He didn't need to say it. I know she is.

Then we all hugged again and Bugsy made me laugh big time because he jumped up and got Pearl's salmon-pink jacket all dirty. I made this HILARIOUS comment about how the jacket looked better that way and you should have seen Pearl's face. She was FUMING. It was great.

Anyway, the point is, I meant it earlier. Not the bit about Pearl's jacket. The bit about how we're family now. The six of us together. Patrice, Dad, Pearl, me, Rosy and Bugsy. And we're going to be just fine. Isn't that right, Pearl?

At last. One thing we can agree on.

CHAPTER TWENTY-TWO

"Why are you hiding?"

I jump at Izzy's voice, spinning round to see her standing right behind me.

"I'm admiring this giant cake," I say innocently, gesturing at the four-tiered, white-iced extravaganza in front of me.

"You're *hiding* behind the giant cake," she corrects. "It wouldn't be because everyone is on the dancefloor now, would it? Because from what I remember from that time we were trying to disturb all the meetings in the house, you were pretty good at dancing."

"Very funny." I frown. "There's no need for sarcasm."

"Who's being sarcastic?" Izzy shrugs.

I don't believe her, but I decide to end the debate there, and instead we look across the room at the dancefloor where Mum and Jackson are having the time of their lives, officially married three hours ago. Jackson spins Mum round and she throws her head back and laughs before he pulls her back towards him, giving her a big kiss on the lips. Everyone around them cheers.

"Gross," Izzy says, wrinkling her nose.

"Disgusting," I agree, shuddering.

We catch each other's eye and smile. It's nice to know what the other one's thinking without saying it out loud: our parents are happy again, everything is as it should be.

Mum looks beautiful in her wedding dress, an off-the-shoulder satin gown designed by Vivienne Westwood, and Jackson, I must say, looks very handsome in his tux. It's really nice to see everyone so dressed up and letting their hair down for the day. Beth and Gabrielle are up with the DJ, trying their best to take over the music, Tony is busy shimmying across the dancefloor like a modern-day Frank Sinatra, the Health Minister is exceptional at the robot, and who knew the Chancellor of the Exchequer was so good at the limbo? Even Maya, who is still on duty heading up Mum's security for the day, has pinned a cheery rose to her usual black jacket and earlier I saw her bopping her shoulders before she caught me looking.

Sebastian isn't on the dancefloor because he was

NOT invited to the wedding. He was, however, invited by Mum to have a cup of tea and talk everything through once she and Jackson are back from their honeymoon. Mum is all about second chances and maintains that he did have some good qualities. She thinks that he just got a bit lost, swallowed up in his own ambition. Since he left, he's discovered he has just one supporter, Preeya, and she backtracked pretty sharpish.

He humbly accepted the invitation for tea.

"Good riddance, I say," the Chancellor of the Exchequer told Izzy and me the other day when we were all putting on our rollerblades for a quick skate around the block before her next meeting with Mum. "I never liked him."

"Neither did we," Izzy said with a sigh. "Patrice wants to forgive him."

"*If* he's sorry," I added.

"Don't worry, you two," the Chancellor said, tightening the helmet strap under her chin. "I'll make sure he's sorry all right. And trust me, it will be worse than a whack about the head with a canapé tray."

Izzy and I made a note never to get on her bad side.

Strangely, thanks to Sebastian, Mum's job is safer than ever. Because of her honest, off-the-cuff speech about family, her support went through the roof and, since then, she's become more and more popular. His plan backfired spectacularly.

Bugsy and Rosy have, of course, been a big part of the wedding day. They were specially groomed for the occasion, which was HILARIOUS, because Bugsy emerged from the groomer looking like a completely different dog. His hair was so fluffy and soft compared to his normal scraggly look that we almost didn't recognize him. Izzy was appalled and made sure that he was a bit less prim by the time of the service by running him round the garden a few times.

Izzy and I are bridesmaids, which I have reminded Izzy a million times is a great privilege.

"Bridesmaids," Izzy repeated after Mum and Jackson asked us, once the wedding planning had commenced. "Does that mean I have to wear a stupid dress?"

"Izzy!" I hissed, nudging her to shut up while Mum and Jackson watched on with bemused expressions. "That's not what you say when someone asks you to be a bridesmaid."

"What do you say?"

"You say, 'Thank you very much, I'd be honoured.'"

"Oh. OK. Thank you very much, I'd be honoured," she mumbled.

"*We'd* be honoured," I said, smiling up at Mum.

"But PLEASE can we pick the outfits?" Izzy blurted out, causing Mum and Jackson to laugh and me to roll my eyes.

I swear I roll my eyes a hundred times a day now I live with Izzy again. They moved right back into 10 Downing Street the day after the proposal and things have been going much more smoothly the second time around.

For one thing, it helps that Izzy and I aren't trying to ruin things for everyone now. It means that all the staff and Mum's colleagues are a lot more relaxed. These days, if they see us on the way to meetings they'll high-five us or ask us to wish them luck if they're pitching something important to Mum.

Izzy HAD to completely ignore me and go plant a whoopee cushion in the Cabinet Room a few days after she moved back in, but she's promised to never do it again and apparently it actually went down a treat.

"The Minister of Defence sat on it after a particularly long rant about the state of the country," Mum said, giggling reluctantly as she recalled the incident. "The whole room fell into complete silence and then there was a roar of laughter from him. Everyone else started laughing too and then we just couldn't stop. After that, the meeting was a breeze. I think we all needed the laugh, to be honest."

Izzy did have to do an extra hour of homework as punishment, which she thought was really unfair when her prank had been welcomed, but I told her she got off lightly, especially as she hadn't got in trouble for the whole big dish thing.

We had to tell the police that it miraculously reappeared.

"Have you considered it might have been a ghost?" Izzy said as the detectives scratched their heads in the Cabinet Room. "I heard a rumour there's a spooky three-headed ghost that roams the halls of 10 Downing Street, stealing items and then replacing them as a warning that this is their house and one day they shall exact their revenge. . ."

Mum gave her a warning look and she shut up sharpish.

Tony is so happy to have Izzy back, he threw her a little welcome home party in the kitchen with cake and balloons and everything. Bugsy discovered the best game ever of pouncing on the balloons and bursting them, while Izzy pretended that her eyes weren't welling up as Tony passed her the knife to cut the cake.

He's promised to teach her to play chess well enough to beat me.

Yeah, sure, Tony. Good one.

I can't say our tutors are that happy to have Izzy join us for lessons again. When she popped her head round the door for each tutor, announcing herself by going, "GUESS WHO'S BACK?!", each of them looked genuinely horrified.

But even they have to admit she livens things up a bit.

I wish she was a bit *less* lively at involving me in things without my permission. So far, she's signed me up to local football, netball, tennis and swimming.

"I don't want to go!" I whined as she tied the laces on her trainers before football practice the other day. "It's cold and rainy out."

"Come on, Pearl," she encouraged, jumping to her feet and bouncing round the room. "You have to do things that challenge you! I think that may be a quote from you, right?"

"Yes," I said, irritated. "I said that at an event last week. I think I stole it from Tony, actually, when he was trying to persuade me to be nice to you when you first arrived."

"Practise what you preach! This will be FUN. Look, you didn't want to do rollerblading at first either, did you? Now look at you! You glide like a swan on those blades!"

"I glided into a wall this morning and you know it."

"My point is, you're getting *better*," she insisted. "Let's give this football thing a go and if you hate it, we don't have to go again. Now that you've got me to push you about, you can try new things. You can't lock yourself away in Downing Street for ever."

"But I like it here," I grumbled. "And football looks muddy."

"It says on the website that it's lots of fun, open to all abilities and a great opportunity to make new friends. Those are all positive things, so let's go," she said, jogging out the door, refusing to take no for an answer.

I was TERRIBLE at football. I couldn't kick the ball when it came near me, I refused to tackle anyone in case it made me fall over and ruin my white shorts, and at one point someone on my team PURPOSEFULLY kicked the ball up in the air at my head and then had the audacity to look disappointed in me when I dodged out the way.

"It's called a header," Izzy said, laughing, when I accused my teammate of treason.

By the end of the session, I was cold, muddy and exhausted.

"So, will we see you next week?" the traitorous teammate asked, grinning widely and giving me a clap on the back.

"Yeah," I said, grinning back. "See you next week."

I admit it was a *little* bit fun.

It's strange. Having spent months wishing Jackson and Izzy had never come into my life, I now can't imagine life without them. I've grown so used to getting Izzy's opinion on anything, I'm not very good at making decisions without her. And mealtimes are so much better now that I have people to eat with. When Mum's there – and she does try her best to join us almost every day unless there's something else completely unmissable – we have proper family dinners, and they're so loud and unruly, the exact opposite of what I ever would have wanted. Now, I wouldn't have it any other way.

Jackson and I have spent some proper time together, too, which has been really nice. He's very calm and gentle, but he also has this great sense of humour, apart from the odd dad joke, but you have to let him have those. He was so shocked to hear I've never been to a theme park that he's promised to take me (Izzy roared with laughter at the idea of me on a rollercoaster) and he's started giving me lessons in how to train dogs. Apparently, I'm a natural. ("It's because she's so good at telling people what to do," Izzy said before I threw a dog biscuit at her head.) Jackson said that if I want, I can have a cameo on the next season of his TV show.

Most importantly, he adores Mum and he makes her

happy and that's all that matters to me. It's a real bonus, I guess, that I get a dad, too.

"When do you think we get to eat the wedding cake?" Izzy asks me now, eyeing up the buttercream icing. "I heard the layers are all different flavours."

"They are. Aren't you full from dinner?"

"Stuffed," she admits, patting her tummy. "I'm glad they took some of my suggestions to heart when putting together the menu. It was all delicious."

"Your only suggestion was 'nothing too fancy and gross'." I laugh, shaking my head at her. "I'm not sure you can take credit for tonight's menu."

"Trust me, Pearl, if it wasn't for me we'd have another food-in-the-napkin situation, but luckily that was avoided." She checks the pockets of her skirt and sighs. "I thought I put my phone in here. I want to take a picture of the cake! Must have left it in that stupid clutch you forced me to bring."

You should have seen the fuss Izzy made over our bridesmaid dresses and clutch options when Mum finally got round to organizing them. I'd already created a mood board with ideas and inspiration, which I'm sure Mum found very helpful, but Izzy took one look at it, made a face and went, "What's with all the pastels? Are you *trying* to look like a marshmallow?"

Then she thought it would be a MARVELLOUS idea to come up with her own mood board, which looked as though we were going to a rock concert, not the sophisticated London wedding of the British Prime Minister.

We argued over the boards until Mum stood up abruptly.

"All right, that's enough!" she cried. "Let me ask you a question. Do you know why you two are joined at the hip?"

"We are not joined at the hip!" I argued.

"Yeah. We're completely independent!" Izzy said.

"Come on," Mum sighed, unable to stop a smile creeping over her face, even though I wasn't sure what was so funny. "You two have become inseparable. Everyone knows you're best friends, whether you meant to be or not."

Izzy and I gave each other uneasy looks.

"What's your point?" I huffed.

"Yeah. What's your point?" Izzy repeated.

"I asked you, do you know *why* you're joined at the hip? It's because your differences complement each other!" Mum clapped her hands as though it was obvious all along. "And we will be celebrating those differences in the outfits. So, this is what we're going to do: you two are going to help each other create your perfect bridesmaid looks. Izzy, I want you to help Pearl find an outfit that makes her feel brilliant about herself, and Pearl, I want you to do the same for Izzy. I'll have the final say. How does that sound?"

"That sounds AWESOME," Izzy squealed, holding up her hand so we could high-five.

"Thanks, Mum!" I beamed, deciding to take a proper look at Izzy's mood board. "You know, there are some really cool ideas in here for you, Izzy."

"Yours too! I reckon we need to jazz it up a bit."

"Yeah, but you know I'm not very good with accessories..."

We hadn't noticed Mum sneaking out the room but by the time we looked up, she was gone.

In the end, we agreed on the same colours so that even though we were wearing different outfits, we were still sort of matching; complementing each other just like Mum had said. I found out that Mum's bridal bouquet was going to be a colour palette of burnt orange and red flowers, so I am in a burnt orange wrap-around dress with butterfly sleeves, and Izzy is wearing a high-waisted skirt of the same colour with a white halterneck top. We both have little white flowers in our hair, and matching shoes with a small block heel and satin ribbon that ties up around our ankles. I insisted on adding a matching white clutch with an orange bow on it, because I thought we might need somewhere to keep our phones.

Izzy has, so far, lost her bag four times.

"Let's go dance," Izzy suggests, grabbing my wrist and trying to drag me from my safe spot behind the cake. "I love this song!"

"I'm too scared," I admit, yanking my hand from her grip. "You know I don't like dancing."

"That was before."

"Before what?"

"Before *me*," she says pointedly. "You don't have to be scared because I'll be dancing stupidly right next to you. You won't be on your own."

I glance at the dancefloor. It does look like it's a lot of fun.

"Promise you won't leave me up there alone?" I say sternly.

"I promise." She laughs.

"All right then." I take a deep breath. "Let's go."

"Hi, girls!" The wedding photographer appears from nowhere, holding up her camera. "Can I get a picture? Your parents specifically asked for plenty of you two!"

"Sure thing! But then we're hitting up the dancefloor," Izzy informs her, throwing an arm around me.

"Perfect," the photographer declares as we smile for the flashes. She lowers her camera and checks the pictures, nodding happily. "That's great. Thank you."

"Come on, Pearl!" Izzy exclaims, skipping away towards the dancefloor and bopping her way right into the middle, receiving an enthusiastic welcome from Mum and Jackson before the three of them immediately start looking about for me.

The photographer laughs, nodding towards Izzy. "So, from today you two are officially stepsisters, right?"

"Sisters," I correct, grinning so wide it makes my jaw ache, as my family gesture for me to come join them. "And we have been for a while now."

ACKNOWLEDGEMENTS

A lot has happened over the past year, and the world is forever changing. I believe in people-power and I believe that every now and then a new hero comes along and reshapes the world forever; inspiring a new generation to think bigger, reach higher and aspire to greatness.

Creating this story and these characters represents a dream much bigger than myself; it represents positive change and unity; it represents a diverse world with possibilities. It shows that love wins above anything else and it proves that teamwork literally makes the dream work. I'm very proud of this book and everyone that has helped to shape it and make it happen. I'm surrounded by a team that share my vision, and continue to create books that inspire young readers.

I hope you enjoy. I also hope that one day I live to see the first black female Prime Minister and I secretly hope that behind No.10 there are plenty of shenanigans! :)

A massive thank you to my family, friends and
wonderful team for your love and continued support,
and to the whole team at Scholastic, Lauren Fortune,
Aimee Stewart, Peter Matthews, Georgina Russell,
Rachel Partridge, Penelope Daukes and Catherine Bell.
My incredible agent Lauren Gardner and the one and
only Katy Birchall who brought this story to life!

Happy reading, beautiful people :)

Love always

Alesha X

Photo by Aimee Stewart

KATY BIRCHALL is the author of the side-splittingly funny *Morgan Charmley: Teen Witch* books, *The It Girl: Superstar Geek*, *The It Girl: Team Awkward*, *The It Girl: Don't Tell the Bridesmaid* and the *Hotel Royale* series, *Secrets of a Teenage Heiress* and *Dramas of a Teenage Heiress*. Katy also works as a freelance journalist and has written a non-fiction book, *How to be a Princess: Real-Life Fairy Tales for Modern Heroines*.

Katy won the 24/7 Theatre Festival Award for Most Promising New Comedy Writer with her very serious play about a ninja monkey at a dinner party.

Katy's first novel for adults, *The Secret Bridesmaid*, published in May 2021.

Look out for *How Not to be a Vampire Slayer* this autumn.

DON'T MISS ALESHA'S HIGH-VOLTAGE, LAUGH-OUT-LOUD, MEGA-BESTSELLING LIGHTNING GIRL SERIES!

Photo by John Wright

IMAGINE SWAPPING LIVES WITH YOUR
FAVOURITE POP STAR…